REVIEW AND HERALD® PUBLISHING ASSOCIATION
HAGERSTOWN, MD 21740

The author assumes full responsibility for the accuracy of all facts and quotations as cited in this book.

This book was
Edited by Gerald Wheeler
Cover designed by Leumas Design/Willie Duke
Interior designed by Freshcut Design
Cover art by Getty Images
Typeset: Usherwood 11/14

PRINTED IN U.S.A.

08 07 06 05 04 5 4 3 2 1

R&H Cataloging Service
Booth, Bradley Stephen, 1957-
Witnesses to the execution: a story of the crucifixion.

1. Jesus Christ—Crucifixion. I. Title.

232.96

ISBN 0-8280-1767-0

Dedication

I want to dedicate this book to my parents,
Herbert and Esther Booth,
who inspired me to search for Jesus
with all my heart and soul and mind.
Today my parents rest in their graves,
but will one day be called forth to meet Jesus,
who is the resurrection and the life.

CONTENTS

Chapter One - FRIDAY / **9**

Chapter Two - SABBATH / **14**

Chapter Three - SUNDAY / **23**

Chapter Four - MONDAY / **30**

Chapter Five - TUESDAY / **38**

Chapter Six - WEDNESDAY / **47**

Chapter Seven - THURSDAY / **55**

Chapter Eight - FRIDAY / **62**

Chapter Nine - SABBATH / **71**

Chapter Ten - SUNDAY / **82**

Chapter Eleven - THREE WEEKS LATER / **89**

Chapter One

FRIDAY

The sounds of insects and other creatures serenaded the cool night like a young mother lulling her child to sleep. It was the third hour of the evening watch. Malachi leaned over the parapet of the rooftop room he had rented for the week and gazed out across Jerusalem, bathed by the Passover moon. For centuries the ancient city had been a center of commerce, political tension, and zealous worship of the one true God.

Jerusalem was the cosmopolitan home of traveling merchants, religious sects such as the Pharisees and Sadducees, and, of course, craftspeople, vendors, and innkeepers. For the most part, the farmers and shepherds kept to themselves in the villages and fields of the surrounding countryside, but now and then they wandered into the city to peddle their livestock and produce.

Even at this late hour Malachi could see that some of the city's occupants just would not call it a day. A few wealthy young men still searched the moonlit streets for adventure and mischief. Here and there an old man lingered under the archway of some door to talk with his fellow crony. Now and then an occasional wandering oil lamp flickered in the darkness of a shadowed street, and somewhere in the night Malachi could hear the yelping of one of the scavenger dogs as a hapless passerby stumbled over it.

From his vantage point atop the rooftop balcony Malachi could see the city sprawling its way up toward the north. Across the acres of rooftops he could clearly make out the Roman soldiers standing in the flickering torchlight as they guarded the walls of Herod's former palace and the Antonia Fortress. The bray of pack animals hinted that out on the Damascus road a few dawdling travelers approached the city. Malachi smiled to himself. Surely they must know that they would probably have to spend the night outside the city gate. The city authorities seldom opened the gates after dark—except perhaps during the Passover.

Malachi clucked his tongue and shook his head in disbelief. As a merchant he knew only too well the hazards that plagued such travelers. Bandits on the road at this hour did not make welcome companions. For all those still out there at this hour, he could only pray that no harm would befall them.

And the Sabbath had begun hours ago. "They must be Gentiles," Malachi muttered. "Or irreverent Jews." One or the other, for neither would consider traveling on the Sabbath to be of much consequence.

It should be no surprise. With the Romans occupying the land nothing about the Jewish way of life could ever be sacred or secure. Their general disregard for all that Malachi and his people considered holy made them a curse to everyone and everything in the Jewish world.

The Roman authorities and soldiers did what they wanted and took what they pleased. They could commandeer a horse or pack animal if they wished, or rip your cloak off your back. Why, they could even take the lunch right out of your mouth if they so desired.

An annoying moth fluttered persistently around Malachi's face, searching for warmth. He brushed it away impatiently and sighed. Would the Messiah never come? Would Israel ever be free of the oppressive Romans who monitored every move that the inhabitants of Jerusalem made in its streets?

And taxes? It seemed as if the Romans had a tax collector on every street corner, and penalties were heavy if you couldn't or wouldn't pay. Malachi winced as he thought of all the bribes he had had to pay as a prosperous merchant back home in Caesarea. It had been a major task during the last year just keeping the local tax collector off his back—several tax collectors, actually. There was the tax collector in his own neighborhood and the one who had jurisdiction over the shops in the merchant district of Caesarea. Oh, and of course he must not forget the governor's own tax official who regularly came looking for under-the-table bribes on goods imported from outside the country.

Occupiers, that was what the Romans were—and empire

builders. Entering a new region, they would conquer it and then set up a new government, new laws, and new culture. The Roman citizens had all the rights as they brought in their shrines and slaves and money. It was a whole new way of life for everyone.

And Jerusalem had its own set of problems. Maybe that was because it was the religious center of the Jewish culture. Although the Romans did allow a puppet form of government to operate under the auspices of the Temple, they always had several garrisons of soldiers stationed in and around the vicinity. Malachi was glad that he didn't have to deal with such powerful civil and religious tensions where he lived.

Not that Caesarea was much better off than Jerusalem. The Jews and Gentiles didn't exactly get along there, either (Caesarea was a predominately Gentile city) but Malachi had learned to make his business work for him, both economically and socially. Traveling frequently, from time to time he came up to Jerusalem on business. It was a good life. He was a merchant of fine tapestries and carpets—some said he possessed the finest stock in the region.

But tonight he was in Jerusalem on business other than commerce. He was here searching—on a quest, one might say. Certain rumors had intrigued Malachi for some time—stories of a miraculous healer named Jesus from Nazareth in Galilee. The man had become quite popular during the past few years and a spiritual leader of sorts. There were those who touted him as a revolutionary in some sense of the word. Others were calling him teacher and rabbi. His most faithful supporters referred to him simply as Master. But the real question—was he the Promised One, the long-looked-for Messiah?

Malachi had heard that Jesus was losing ground with the Jewish leadership in Jerusalem, and that if he was going to make a prominent political move, he would have to do it soon. This latest rumor had reached Caesarea, prompting a deployment of several more squadrons of soldiers to the Roman Praetorian in Jerusalem.

Other rumors circulated that were not so believable, such as the account Malachi had heard of Jesus walking on water up there on the Sea of Tiberias in Galilee. Probably some bogus tale hatched around the evening campfires of shepherds and caravan travelers or a last-ditch effort by his followers to increase his popularity with the masses. And then there were the stories of his feeding thousands, they said, with a single basket of food. Simple peasant food—a few fish and loaves—but food nevertheless, and thousands had shared it. Believable, as far as miracles of God were concerned? Maybe. Authentic? Probably not.

But the story of late that had really taken the region by storm involved Jesus' raising a man back to life. Oh, Malachi had heard such stories before, but to him they were the stuff of folk tales and legends. Just idle talk. As a business person Malachi's tried-and-true policy had always been, "If you show me the goods, then I can buy the merchandise." Stories were nice, but as for himself, Malachi had to be able to see something before he could believe in it.

And yet this latest incident sounded pretty reliable. Scores of people had seen the miracle—right there at the tomb just a few days before, somewhere just beyond Jerusalem's walls. Someone had been in a tomb for four days, and then been raised to life again. Walked right out of the tomb. It was earth-shattering in its implications—if it was actually true!

And that was the biggest question of all, wasn't it? That was the problem. If the story was true—if any of these stories could be confirmed—then maybe Malachi would have something on which to pin his wavering hope for a Messiah. But how does one go about proving some wild tale to be true?

Well, Malachi had pondered the dilemma again and again during the several weeks prior to this trip to Jerusalem. Once and for all, if he wanted to get to the bottom of the quandary that had been tormenting his heart for so long now, he was just going to have to track down the stories. He had to find out for himself.

Hearsay wasn't good enough for him. Never had been. When he got a thing in his head, he had to sort it out, sift through all the whys and wherefores, and then search out the real story back to its origin. Then, and only then, could he reach a conclusion based on all the evidence. Kind of philosophical, Malachi guessed, but it worked for him.

He shivered in the cool night air. A mist had begun to settle on the lower regions of the city, but the wind was bringing the murky chill of the evening's dampness up and across the rooftops.

Absentmindedly Malachi pulled his cloak tighter around him. He had given his investigation quite a bit of thought. To do it right, he would have to find credible people who could give him verifiable, genuine accounts of the miracle man in action. Witnesses were what Malachi needed, like in a court of law at the city gate. He must find people who could testify as to where Jesus had come from, probe their impressions of who He really was. It wouldn't be easy.

So that was Malachi's mission, if he had the courage to go through with it. He felt that he needed to find the truth—at least that was what he thought he really wanted. The question was, What if he wasn't happy with the truth?

What if this man called Jesus did turn out to be the Messiah? That was something Malachi had always thought he really wanted, but would Jesus be the kind of Messiah everybody hoped for? Somebody that would meet their expectations?

The evening starlight winked sleepily above as the nocturnal concert ebbed and then surged on into the night. Somewhere above in the sky a night bird whistled it's way on an evening hunt.

Malachi went to his pallet and stretched out under the stars. It was a cloudless night. Despite the chill he would sleep out of doors. Maybe the night sky would clear his mind and give him a better perspective on the exciting, yet overwhelming task ahead of him. He hoped so.

Chapter Two

SABBATH

Malachi paused at the imposing courtyard gate and shook the dust from the folds of his robe. Beads of perspiration dotted his forehead as he glanced about, searching for some telltale sign that he had arrived at the residence he was looking for.

A sparrow flitted to the twisted tendrils of a grapevine winding it's way up the courtyard wall. The bird whistled a simple tune, and then cocked its head to one side as though it were on some type of an inspection tour. "Hello, little one," Malachi said gently, his voice suddenly awed at the delicate features of the tiny bird. "You certainly don't appear as if you have a care in the world."

Amazing, Malachi thought, that a creature so small could survive long enough to be carefree and sing its little songs. He smiled at the little fellow, then turned his mind to the business at hand.

In a rich baritone cadence he began to chant a Hebrew Sabbath day's blessing for those inside the gate. His voice rose and fell on the warm afternoon air like a drifting butterfly until a servant girl appeared. She opened a little sliding door in the gate. "Shalom, friend. The master of the house wishes to know who is calling."

"Tell him I wish to speak to him of Jesus," Malachi replied.

The girl's eyebrows raised in question until he added, "Jesus of Nazareth." After all, Jesus was a common name.

She disappeared, only to return a few minutes later. "The rabbi will see you now."

Malachi entered a courtyard of flowering vines and shrubbery. Exotic birds twittered in cages hung from the ceiling of a balcony overlooking the courtyard.

The rabbi arrived moments later. His expensive robes revealed his position, and a silver-streaked beard gave him the dignity of a patriarch. He was short and still in middle life, but like many of the more affluent in Jerusalem, he ate well.

Malachi came straight to the point. "Blessings to you, Rabbi. My name is Malachi, son of Obed. I'm a merchant from Caesarea, a retailer of carpets and tapestries, but it is Jesus of Nazareth that I have come to speak to you about."

The religious leader studied him. "Do you know Jesus of Nazareth?"

"Only what I've heard of him—I've never met him personally. I was hoping you could tell me more about him."

Malachi thought the rabbi looked a bit indignant. Was he wasting the man's time? It was obvious that one had to be important to even get into the rabbi's home.

The older man studied Malachi carefully, as though scrutinizing his intentions. He paused to take in the clothes Malachi was wearing, the cut of his hair, the money pouch tucked in his belt. Finally he decided that his visitor appeared sincere enough. "I know the man." The rabbi's reply surprised Malachi. "Actually, he is scheduled to be here shortly. At the moment I couldn't tell you where he is exactly. Somewhere between here and Jerusalem, I imagine. Probably on one of his Sabbath tours to teach and heal."

The rabbi smiled at Malachi and settled himself heavily on a bench under the shade of a mulberry tree. "Please make yourself comfortable," he added, gesturing to a spot on the bench beside him. "You didn't journey far, I trust? Such a thing is not customary in Israel on the Sabbath, as I'm sure you know."

"No, of course not." Malachi sensed a note of displeasure in the rabbi's voice when he spoke of Sabbath observance and Jesus. *But the rabbi is right,* Malachi mused. The Torah forbade long journeys on the Sabbath, but according to contemporary Jewish law, it was more than just banned—it was criminal. Somehow the rabbi disapproved of Jesus' behavior, Malachi realized, and he could understand that. But the religious leader's reaction also puzzled him. The merchant had asked an innkeeper whom he should see in order to learn more about this Jesus. Although Malachi had hoped that the rabbi would be a positive lead, now he wondered if contacting him hadn't been such a good idea after all. He would try one more time.

Malachi cleared his throat. "So if this Jesus of Nazareth leaves his home on Sabbath and his journeys take him far and wide, then—"

"Ah, yes. Jesus and the Sabbath," the rabbi interrupted with a frown. "Jesus is out, somewhere, on more than what one might call a Sabbath day's journey. But then again, Jesus of Nazareth seems to do as he pleases on the Sabbath. If there's any one thing that distinguishes him from others, it's his own personal sense of what is appropriate on the Sabbath day." The rabbi shook his head incredulously. "If you haven't discovered that by now, you probably soon will."

He took a seed from a basket beside him and offered it to a rose-ringed parakeet in a nearby cage of iron. The beautiful green bird with its narrow pink collar eagerly snatched the food. "What do you want with Jesus? Is there someone sick in your family?"

"No—actually, I've just been hoping to find out a little more about him. I've heard that his popularity has taken a turn for the worse as of late, at least with the leaders of the Sanhedrin. That's why I came to you. I thought that since you are a close friend of his, you might be able to help me out."

"Close friends?" The rabbi raised his eyebrows. "I wouldn't exactly say that we're close, but that's beside the point. You're right about his popularity with the priests. With the common people it's a different story, but the priests and Pharisees . . ."

With a sigh the rabbi paused to watch the shifting patterns the leaves of an almond tree made on the ground. "Jesus of Nazareth delights in the good he can do on the Sabbath," the rabbi continued. "That's what gets him into so much trouble. Our opinion—well, at least that of most of the Pharisees—is that he is far from orthodox in theory or practice. He is unpredictable, nontraditional, and most certainly irregular in his methods." The rabbi frowned again. "And he is not satisfied with confining his healing ministry to a mere six days of the week. He insists on healing during the Sabbath hours too, and that often involves a lot of travel time as well as a lot of—unnecessary healing."

"Unnecessary healing?" Malachi knew he sounded surprised.

The rabbi avoided his visitor's searching gaze by turning to the parakeet to give him another seed. "Yes, healing that could wait until another day of the week." The rabbi appeared a bit impatient at

Malachi's apparent ignorance of such matters, but mostly at his incessant questioning.

"Ritual cleansing for the body because of illness takes place day in and day out at the Temple," the religious official added, "but we do not offer those services on the Sabbath day. God did not intend the Sabbath for such things. We should not clutter it with the busy work of sinners and their maladies, when they could just as well seek healing on another day. The Sabbath was made for Temple officials, too, you know. We need our rest as well." Although the rabbi spoke authoritatively, he still appeared troubled.

Malachi stared intently at him. "You've a point, but healing people—I mean, if his miracles are from heaven, can one really tell God when to perform them and when not to? Doesn't God pretty much do as He pleases?"

The rabbi shifted uncomfortably. "That would be a good rule to live by," he countered, "if Jesus would leave it up to God." The rabbi sounded irritated. Not angry, just irritated. He squinted at Malachi as though he were attempting to explain the obvious to a simple child.

"What I'm referring to is Jesus' obsession with forgiveness, his habit of handing out forgiveness as though it were free. Why, he has made forgiveness in these parts as commonplace as the air we breathe. Hands it out as though he were God himself. And what's worse, he offers it to people who don't deserve it—the terminally ill, for example. I mean, some of the most wretched souls that come to us deserve to be ill because of the lives they've led. It's obvious that God has put His curse upon them as punishment for their lives of wickedness."

Malachi had heard such sentiments before, but he had never been comfortable with them. Of course, he didn't have to deal with the issue on a daily basis as the rabbi did.

The rabbi hurried on. "It's like this. When someone comes to the Temple to receive a clean bill of health from an illness, we wait until we see the obvious signs of healing before we declare them completely forgiven by God. To do otherwise is simply presumptuous. But, you see," he continued, "Jesus offers the forgiveness to them first. I mean, it's as if he already knows that God is going to heal them before the fact—or something."

"Jesus does all this?"

"He does." The rabbi frowned again, then added hastily, "It's all a bit confusing, I guess. On the one hand, as religious leaders we try to offer our worshipers a healthy blend of sacred Scripture and holy traditions sent down to us from our ancestors. And then Jesus comes along and offers a more radical view of God. His Father—that's the term he uses most often, I believe, and he makes their relationship look so simple, so unassuming."

The rabbi shook his head slowly, then fidgeting with the basket of seeds in his lap, he hurriedly added, "But forgiveness, and the right to offer it freely to everyone, is available only from God. No man has the right to assume that role. Such a pretense on anyone's part is blasphemy. You must know that, I'm sure."

He hesitated a moment at the sound of his own words before continuing. "That's what we've always believed and professed." The rabbi said it as if he was trying to convince himself, yet sensing that something was not quite right.

Malachi ignored the rabbi's confusion. "But now?"

The rabbi looked down at his feet self-consciously. "But now Jesus has threatened all of that—or so it seems. The common people no longer look to us as the authority on such things. The fact is, at the moment Jesus has more influence with them than we do. He eats and drinks with them, associates with them, consorts with them. I can assure you that it's done nothing for his image with the Sanhedrin."

Malachi thought the rabbi looked sad, almost wistful, as he leaned forward and set the basket of seeds down on the rough paving stones of the courtyard. "I think things would be a lot better for Jesus if he were a little more conventional. If he would just stop being so contrary, He could have anything he wanted—anything at all. Fame. Fortune. Position. Power."

The religious leader lapsed into silence. The late afternoon had grown warmer, but Malachi remained oblivious to everything else. All he cared about at the moment was to find out more about Jesus. The parakeet on its perch cocked his head to one side as though he, too, was waiting to hear about the miracle worker.

"And what do you think of Jesus, personally?" Malachi probed.

The rabbi brushed a few seed fragments off his lap and stood. He leaned his shoulder against the trunk of a gnarled old olive tree and sighed as he gazed out over the courtyard wall at the Mount of Olives rising from the Kidron Valley below. "What do I think of him personally?" He stroked his beard pensively, and his eyes had a far away look as if he were peering through a window into another time and place.

"I guess if I'm to be honest, I"—he paused, then began again. "If you had asked me that two years ago, I would have been direct in my reply—quite direct. Back then I hardly knew him—not the way the ordinary people did. With the heritage of his Galilean hill country stamped on his sun-bronzed features, he seemed ordinary enough. Hardly one to be reckoned with. But of course that was then."

"And something has happened to change all that now?" Malachi ventured.

"It has," the rabbi replied meekly. "I guess you could say that he's given me a new lease on life."

"A new lease?"

"Yes, but it's more than that." The rabbi appeared a bit embarrassed at his own explanation. "It's—it's the effect Jesus continues to have on me whenever I'm around him."

Malachi leaned toward him.

The rabbi searched his visitor's face for any trace of insincerity, but he saw only genuine interest and an honest searching for truth.

"It's the way he looks at me," the rabbi continued. "The way I feel when his gaze fastens upon me—it's as though his thoughts were piercing through my very soul. As if he knows the deepest secrets of my life."

The merchant sensed an undercurrent in the rabbi, as though some sort of transformation had suddenly come over him. Before, he had sounded cynical, even bitter—now he was almost submissive.

With a shrug the rabbi sighed. "In spite of my disapproval of some of the things Jesus does, I guess I find myself irresistibly drawn to him." His voice was unapologetic. "You would know what I'm talking about, Malachi, if you could meet him. If you met him even once, you would understand completely what I am trying to tell you." Again he sighed heavily as though he was trying to roll a great burden from off his chest.

"You know, it's funny," he added with a look of chagrin. "Men of my profession never lack for words. It's in our blood to dispute and debate, to argue, to persuade. All my life I have been trained to find discrepancies in the claims of revolutionaries such as Jesus. I should have lots more to say in defense of my position and for all that is at stake here. But I don't." The rabbi just shook his head in disbelief. "Just look at me! In many ways I still hardly know the man, yet I find myself more and more expecting him to be the one all Israel has been waiting for. It's incredible!"

Malachi stared disbelievingly at him. "Are you saying that you think this Jesus is the Messiah?"

The rabbi's reply came slowly as though he had spent many hours in this very garden struggling to find words to express the conclusion that he had come to. "Many are saying he has to be, and I say that if he is, then that fact will no doubt soon reveal itself. It's inevitable, to my way of thinking."

Several minutes of silence passed as the two men basked in the waning hours of the day. A butterfly flitted from one large blossom to another.

"And what will you do about this Jesus?" Malachi finally asked, sensing the rabbi's seriousness. "I mean, a person of your position and influence can't afford just to abandon everything to follow him—can you?"

The rabbi smiled instinctively. "Probably not. However, maybe he will come to me. After all, he did accept my invitation readily enough. Perhaps he has finally realized that the backing of a man of my influence can place real power at his fingertips. Perhaps . . ." The rabbi had that faraway look in his eyes again. "It's possible that tonight may be the beginning of something great. That would be ideal, wouldn't it?"

"Tonight?"

"Why not? I have invited him to my house for a feast and a celebration. It's in his honor, of course—I must show Jesus how much his gift of life has meant to me." A sense of contentment relaxed the religious leader's face.

"What is this gift of life you speak of?" Malachi asked.

The rabbi hung his head and then straightened his shoulders to look Malachi full in the face. He answered slowly, searching for words. "It's hard . . . for a man of my profession to reveal the secrets in his life, but I guess I owe you a complete explanation. I've come this far; I might as well let you know the rest." He shuddered. "I still lay awake nights thinking—what I am now—what I almost was. I contracted leprosy, Malachi. Can you believe it? Me, a Pharisee—Simon of the Sanhedrin, a leper—and Jesus healed me!" Slowly he shook his head. "What can I say?"

"Leprosy!" Malachi repeated the word as though it were a deadly poison on his lips.

"That's right," the rabbi admitted. "I was face to face with living death, but Jesus in his compassion healed me of the dreaded disease. Come to think of it, that business about forgiveness must certainly apply to me, too. I can't say that I deserve it, but Jesus gave it to me anyway." Simon nodded his head gently. "So I guess this feast is my way of thanking him—for now, at least."

The older man took another deep breath, then stood. He rubbed his hands together briskly. "And we will do it right! We will spare no pains to make Jesus feel he is among friends. The guest roster was full long ago with every person of prominence in the area, and then some." Slowly he smiled. "Yes, indeed. This celebration will be the talk of the town, I'm certain. A celebration to end all celebrations." He paused. "Can you join us? I'm sure we could make room for just one more."

Malachi wasn't sure whether the invitation was genuine or simply an afterthought. "Oh, thank you, but no. That would be an honor indeed, but I have an invitation elsewhere. I am to dine with an important merchant in Jerusalem this evening. In fact, I had better be going. My contact with the man this evening promises to be a lucrative one financially, so I dare not miss it." He rose to his feet. "But please accept my grateful appreciation for your kind offer."

"Very well!" The rabbi clapped his hands together, and within moments several servants appeared. "I'd better be going, too," he announced. "The family will be gathering shortly. There is much to do. Evening prayers must be said, and then lamps must be lit—and food is to be prepared. You understand, of course."

Smiling once again, he bowed slightly and extended an open hand. "I'm sorry you can't join us, Malachi, but thank you for this pleasant visit. It has been good for me."

Simon showed his visitor to the gate. "If you have any more questions, please feel free to drop by again." He put his hand on Malachi's shoulder. "Perhaps we can visit a little later in the week sometime. The three of us perhaps. We'll share a meal, you and I—and Jesus. Or better yet, we could get together after the Passover. With all that's required of me in Jerusalem, I'll be lucky if I even get a chance to see my own shadow."

Chapter Three

SUNDAY

The sun still lay sleepily under the dim horizon as Malachi stood at the brow of the Mount of Olives overlooking Jerusalem. Below him stretched the pale outline of the Temple complex. And below it stretched the Kidron Valley with its olive groves and vineyards still shrouded in darkness. As the sky behind him turned pink and orange and then saffron yellow, the shadows of dawn crept slowly into the cracks and crevices of a new day.

Malachi stretched his arms high over his head and then slowly rubbed the stiff muscles of his neck. He scratched at several welts on his back. Sleeping in a strange bed had never been his idea of fun. Evidently other creatures had shared it with him.

No matter. Malachi needed to be up anyway. He hadn't slept much thinking about what Rabbi Simon had told him the evening before. If what the religious leader said was true, then the healer and teacher from Nazareth could possibly be the Messiah. The very idea filled him with a strange excitement.

And there had to be others like Simon who could give him a clearer picture of what Jesus' real mission was. Others who knew him well enough to make an honest appraisal at least.

That explained Malachi's presence on a lonely trail at the crack of dawn somewhere west of Bethany.

The woman who had given him directions had told him that the person he was looking for would most likely be at a certain place on the Mount of Olives. "A sacred family spot," she had called it. Usually he went there before sunrise.

I hate to disturb anyone's time with God, Malachi thought, *but it being Passover, if I don't find him early, he'll be gone for the day, and then I'll never catch up with him.*

Malachi crawled over a stone wall and stopped to catch his

breath. *Just where did she say that he might be?* He frowned as he snagged his sleeve on some brambles. *Near their family tomb?* When he yanked his arm free from the thorns he tore several holes in his tunic. Dots of blood appeared immediately on the back of his hand where thorns had punctured his skin. He tried to wipe the blood from his hand, but only smeared it in the process. *Why can't they make the path a little more accessible?* he fumed to himself. *How hard would it be just to cut away some of these brambles, anyway?*

In his frustration Malachi began to doubt the wisdom of his early morning search. Perhaps it was all just a wild-goose chase. He paused to sit on a rock and strained his eyes to search the garden below him. In the shadows he finally spotted the shape of a man in a position of prayer.

That must be him, Malachi concluded—unless, of course, it was a thief. Even the holy city of Jerusalem was full of bandits who roamed the night, preying on the wealthy and the pilgrims who arrived for the yearly festivals. Also he was in an area where many had excavated family tombs in the cliff faces. That would attract robbers to those tombs belonging to the wealthiest families. Sometimes families buried jewelry and valuable items with their loved ones.

When gravel crunched under Malachi's feet, the shadowy figure turned suddenly and stealthily drew something from the folds of his robe. "Who is it?" his voice demanded.

Malachi gulped and caught his breath. Whoever it was must have assumed that Malachi was stalking him. The object he clenched in his hand had to be a dagger.

"A friend," Malachi responded shakily. "I'm a friend. A merchant. Malachi is my name—son of Obed—from the city of Caesarea. I was at your home early this morning, and I was told that I could probably find you here. Your sister, I believe it was, suggested that I would find you here."

The figure in the shadows emerged, his cream-colored robe turning a faint rose from the approaching dawn. He pulled his hood aside, revealing gentle eyes and a bronze beard with faint streaks of red.

"I'm sorry to have disturbed you. I hope I didn't frighten you," Malachi said.

"What do you need?"

"I was hoping I could talk to you about Jesus of Nazareth." The merchant spoke with more confidence than he felt. "I have heard stories—rumors—and I have come a long way to see if they are true."

"Rumors?" The young man returned the short dagger to its place.

As Malachi searched the man's face he saw only honesty and an unassuming demeanor. "Yes, rumors that he claims to be the Messiah. Some say so, at least, and rumors that he has performed a mighty miracle for you."

"And you? What do you believe?"

"I don't know what I believe," Malachi said, raising his hands in helplessness. "What others have told me, I suppose, but it—it's just not enough to . . ." his voice trailed off.

"It isn't enough, is it?" came the soft reply. "You feel the need to search this thing through for yourself. I don't blame you. As a searcher of truth, you feel a need to leave no stone unturned. That's what it is." Without waiting for a response, he continued, "For months now you have probably thought about all that you have gleaned from conversations with friends and strangers alike, and yet you are still unconvinced."

His uncanny ability to grasp Malachi's thoughts and motives was amazing. Again he studied the young man's face, now bathed in the rosy glow streaming down over the crest of the Mount of Olives. He met Malachi's gaze unwaveringly.

"You are close to this Jesus?"

The other man's answer was soft-spoken, yet equally as direct as the question. "Yes, we're friends—very dear friends. I would do anything for the Master. I think that I would even die for him, if that is what he would ask of me."

"Then you are one of the twelve?"

"No. No, I am not—not that I wouldn't want to be. I am a disciple, but not one of the twelve. I have never asked the Master why he has not called me to that group. It is not for me to question, only to serve."

"Tell me all you know about him."

"All I know?" The young man's eyes smiled. "Come, friend. Have a seat." He gestured toward a nearby stone bench. "What I know would take moments. What I have experienced could take days—weeks.

"I'll do my best," he said solemnly and without hesitation. "The Master is the kindest, most compassionate person I have ever met. He is the very essence of goodness and love. And shouldn't he be? After all, he is the Son of God."

A delicate butterfly stirred on the blossoms of a flowering bramble nearby. The man paused briefly to reach his finger toward its gossamer wings. "Of course," he added, turning to Malachi, "His divinity remains for you to discover for yourself. However, if you could travel with him on his missionary journeys as I have, you would see whole villages benefit from the touch of his hand. Whole villages, mind you. Often we walk through towns from one end to the other, and its inhabitants bring their sick out into the streets so that Jesus can minister to them as he passes. He makes those who are blind see, those who are deaf hear. I have seen dozens receive the power to stand on legs that have not walked for years."

A tone of awe filled his voice. "And through it all," he said quietly, "Jesus never lets fatigue or hunger keep him from the people. At times I sense his desperate need to get away from the crowds and the antagonistic Temple officials, but he never lets them prevent him from doing just one more loving act of service to a child of God in need." The hint of a smile curled at the corners of his mouth. "We usually have to beg the Master to take time to rest."

Malachi had a list of questions that he had planned to ask, but now he decided it better just to let the young man follow his own thoughts. It was obvious that he was reliving events that he would treasure the rest of his life. Tilting his head back, the younger man closed his eyes for a moment before continuing. "Not long ago I was with the Lord when we passed through the valley of the lepers. I'll never forget the experience. I think I can honestly say that it was probably the most repulsive place I've ever been." Shaking his head, he glanced at Malachi with a look of self-conscious shame. "I knew I would not be able to look at them for the stench and the grotesqueness of their disease-ravaged features."

For a moment he shivered as if to shake off the memory of it all, and a look of anguished horror crossed his face. "The place was death itself," he groaned. "I thought we must surely be at the very gates of hell."

He took a deep breath. "I feel terrible saying it, but I have never been able to think of lepers as being children of Abraham, stricken as they are with the evil disease, but—" The young man took another deep breath. "But Jesus could. And he did. I think it is just a natural part of him—part of his bond with both his Father and the human race. He walked among the lepers and touched them and called them by name. The rest of us just waited at the entrance to the leper colony. And Malachi—he made some of them over again like newborn babies. Pink-skinned, and sweet-smelling, and fresh." The young man smiled at that part of the memory. "It seemed as if we then soared from the gates of hell to the gates of heaven."

A look of sadness crossed his face as he contemplated yet another memory. "You know, I believe Jesus would have gone throughout the entire colony if people would have wanted him to. Passed through the entire place and healed every one of those rotting corpses huddling there—if they had wanted him to."

The young man's eyes glistened with tears. "And they wouldn't even have had to ask Jesus to do it. If they could have just had the slightest longing deep down inside, the Master would have done it. Gladly. That's his way." The young man swallowed hard, and then disappointment tinged his words. "But they must not have wanted it! They must not have! He could have healed them all, but many of them just kept to themselves in their filthy rags and—and just let him go by!"

His voice broke, and the tears flowed down his face. He wiped them away. Finally he dropped his head to his chest and said nothing more.

Time passed, and Malachi finally stirred. Feeling reluctant to intrude any longer, he decided just to slip away silently. He had come to satisfy his curiosity about rumors of miracles and the man had confirmed them. Malachi would try to content himself with that.

"Please don't go." The young man said as he noticed Malachi rising to leave. "Please. Not yet." His voice had a haunting sadness.

Malachi stared intently him. "You come here often." It was more a statement of fact than a question.

"I do now," the young man confessed. "It is as if something compels me to spend time like this in solitude. I too have met the Master of life and death."

"Your sister mentioned something about you coming here to celebrate a new beginning. A spiritual beginning, perhaps?" Malachi probed.

The younger man nodded. "Yes, I guess you could call it a new beginning." He paused, thinking a moment. "It is somehow difficult to talk about. Not because I'm not grateful," he glanced at Malachi uncertainly. "But because I feel unworthy. And so many people have come to ask me questions just to satisfy their curiosity. I don't mind telling my story if it will honor the Master, but not just to entertain them."

The young man bowed his head again, and then lifted it to gaze at the Temple complex now gleaming in the full morning light. "You've heard the story by now, I'm certain. It seems to have spread everywhere—even, I suppose, to Galilee and back."

"I've heard rumors," Malachi said quietly, "but most of those I've talked to have some doubts." He smiled apologetically. "I just arrived in Jerusalem late last week, so I don't know all the details."

The other man scrutinized Malachi carefully, then exclaimed, "Rumors? How can the miracles of Jesus be mere rumors? There are living testimonies to his power everywhere. Like me, for instance!"

"I've heard bits and pieces," Malachi said hesitantly, uncomfortable in being so direct, "but you know how people love a story. It grows and grows in the repeating, and before long they have embellished it beyond belief." He struggled for words that would mask his skepticism, for a way not to make the situation more awkward. "Of course I—uh—have been here today. I've heard and seen for myself. That makes things considerably different."

The young man laughed, but it was not the sound of amusement. It was a burst of joy. "So you really want to know—want to be open to the Spirit of God? This is wonderful!" he exclaimed almost jubilantly. "At last someone genuinely sincere about his search for truth." He stared at Malachi in wonder. "But will you believe?"

"Believe?" the merchant finally managed to stammer. "I want to believe."

The young man stood to his feet and stretched his arms reverently toward the Judean sky. He pivoted his body around slowly, then began whirling faster and faster in exuberance. "Praise to the Son of David!" he shouted. "The miracle is in this body, my friend. It is the miracle of life which has been given me twice over."

As Malachi stared at the dancing figure before him he tried to fully grasp what the man was saying. "I—I want to believe," the merchant stammered, "but I am a simple man, one who lives by sight. Please, can you help me to believe?"

The younger man halted in front of Malachi. "Let your faith in the power of Jesus help you to take the next step," he said after catching his breath. "By faith just reach out your hand and take mine!" Malachi did as he was told. He extended his hand and grasped the outstretched fingers.

"Now, let your eyes and your hand experience the touch of faith. Only see and believe!" His face aglow with awe, the man proclaimed, "I am living testimony to the divine power of the Jesus who has raised me from death into life."

Like a man caught in a cloudburst in a dry wadi, Malachi felt himself swept along by a flood of emotions. Could it be possible? He felt as if God's presence must be all around him on this early sunlit morning.

"Thank you for coming to see me, Malachi. You have given me a chance to share my testimony to someone who was more than just a curiosity seeker. I am Lazarus, and by God's grace I have returned to the land of the living. Blessed be the name of the Lord!" He smiled again. "I was dead—and am now alive again."

Chapter Four

MONDAY

I've got to see him!" Malachi said impatiently, then paused as if reconsidering. "I mean," he added more diplomatically, "I was sure that the rabbi would see me. I've been told that he and Jesus of Nazareth are friends and have spent a bit of time together." Malachi opened his mouth as if to add something else that might convince the Temple guard, but it was obvious that he wasn't going to make any headway.

"Absolutely not!" The Temple guard was emphatic. "I don't think you understand how busy Temple officials are. This place is like a beehive from before dawn until long after any ordinary person has gone home." The guard set his jaw firmly. "Unless you have a signed and sealed invitation from Rabbi Nicodemus himself, you're not getting past this door."

It was obvious that Malachi had found the right Temple guard—another probably wouldn't even have given him the time of day. However, it was also clear that he would not be allowed to contact the religious leader while the man was still at the Temple.

"Well, thank you anyway." Malachi saluted the guard with a respectful bow. "Here's a little something for your trouble." He dropped a coin into the guard's outstretched hand. "Perhaps I can go to his home—I understand his city residence is not far from here."

"Good luck," the guard shrugged. "I don't run his house, just this little patch of pavement here in the Temple. I follow orders and mind my own business otherwise."

Malachi turned to leave. *What a shame,* he thought. It would have been a real accomplishment to have visited Nicodemus in his chambers here at the Temple itself, rather than at his home. Much more auspicious, and certainly more exciting. No matter. If Rabbi Nicodemus had any credibility at all as a witness, and if indeed he was a friend of the teacher and healer from Galilee, Malachi would find an opportunity to speak with him sooner or later.

There was no use waiting around longer. Malachi snaked his way back through the milling crowd of worshipers, Temple officials, and vendors shouting their wares. The cacophony of bawling, bleating, and cooing of the animals offered for sale as sacrifices signaled one thing to Malachi—a barnyard atmosphere that seemed greatly out of place in the house of God.

Malachi jumped sideways to avoid being stepped on by a young bullock as an irate merchant led it away. "You've swindled me before," the man shouted over his shoulder, "but you'll not do it this time! I'll take the market price you quoted last week, or I'll take nothing at all!"

Someone barked a retort. Malachi couldn't make out the response or who it came from, but it was obvious that the two of them were trading oaths.

Up ahead Malachi could hear a priest in a dispute with a peasant. "You'll have to find another lamb," the priest argued. "That one has an internal blemish."

"I don't see how that's possible," the peasant countered. "I didn't feel any blemish."

"That's because you're not educated in such matters. It takes the trained eye of a Temple official like myself to detect it."

"But I showed the lamb to my wife's cousin in Bethlehem. He works here at the Temple, and he thought it was all right."

The priest was growing impatient now. "I'm sorry, but your wife's—whoever—must have made a mistake. The lamb is clearly unfit for a Temple sacrifice. You'll just have to purchase another."

"But I don't have enough money to buy another lamb!" The peasant's stooped shoulders sagged with discouragement. "I've saved for years to be able to bring a lamb. I'm a poor man, and now when I can finally afford a lamb instead of a turtledove, you tell me—"

"Look! I've made it quite clear what you must do! Take the offer we have made—or leave it. You have no other options!"

Malachi managed a glance at the scene as he passed. The dejected peasant just stood in the middle of the crowd, the lamb's rope leash dangling in his hand. The priest stared at him in stony silence.

Suddenly Malachi felt a heavy hand grab him by the shoulder and spin him around. "You! Come with me!" a gruff voice half shouted over the noise in the Temple.

It was the Temple guard that he had spoken to just minutes before. "Wh—what do you want?" Malachi sputtered in surprise. If he hadn't felt angry at being jerked to a stop, he might have reacted more politely—and maybe been a little bit more worried.

"I don't have further instructions," the guard replied. "Just come with me!"

It looked as though Malachi had no choice but to follow. He tried to keep up with the guard as they pushed their way back through the milling pilgrims in the Temple courtyard. Fortunately the guard made a way for them through the throng. He pushed his way along, shoving the unsuspecting people to the right and left.

The two of them passed the section of the courtyard set up for Temple currency exchange. Malachi frowned at the sight of the men seated behind the tables. Coins clinked, a sure sign of prosperity at some level. *Probably not just for the Temple merchants,* he thought. Demanding that worshipers cash in their street money for Temple currency was an obvious sham—as if ordinary, everyday money was any more defiled or unclean than the blood money some of these Temple personnel exacted from the common people. Yes, the Tyrian shekel had a more consistent weight and purity of silver, but even it had a pagan image on it. *An abominable practice,* Malachi thought. *Just another scheme to get more money into the hands of the powerful.*

And what about the dishonest custom of rejecting perfectly suitable sacrificial animals just to make a few extra shekels? Like the peasant with the lamb—it was an outright shame, and a rude, ungodly practice. Malachi was angry. Where there was money involved, no doubt, someone higher up was taking a cut.

He shook his head in disgust as he tried to keep up with the guard. What must God think of the whole charade? Certainly it was not part of the Lord's original plan for Israel. Malachi couldn't imagine how God's chosen people could have warped the worship experience so badly.

And the noise? It was almost deafening. It made the Temple seem less sacred—somehow, less God-filled—and it just didn't seem right. Had he ever noticed this before? Maybe. But perhaps it had never really been this bad either. He had been to Jerusalem numerous times, and countless times to the Temple, but today it seemed that there was just too much confusion here for anyone's religious experience. And people taking advantage of others in the name of the Lord. The whole thing made him sick to his stomach.

The Temple guard's voice brought Malachi back to the present. "Wait here by the door. I'll be right back."

Moments later, Malachi found himself ushered into a room adorned like a royal palace. He tried not to let his eyes wander, but the opulence of the place was impressive. The plastered walls were painted in brightly colored geometrical patterns, and carefully carved stone tables and ritual storage jars lined the walls. An unusual number of oil lamps relieved the gloom of the windowless room.

"I'm glad you have time for a visit," an authoritative voice said, interrupting Malachi's thoughts. He turned suddenly to face a man robed in expensive garments. "I understand you have asked to speak to Rabbi Nicodemus," the Temple official said.

"Yes," Malachi said, finding his voice. "I did want to see him, but they told me he is not available. I thought I would try his home—maybe I'll have better luck there."

"Rabbi Nicodemus is a busy man," the official continued. "Please, have a seat. Allow my servants to offer you a bit of refreshment." He clapped his hands sharply, and a servant appeared from nowhere with a silver goblet. Another arrived with a small platter arranged with dates, almonds, walnuts, and stone pine seeds.

Malachi nodded his thanks and sampled the delicacies sparingly—he was not sure exactly why the man had summoned him. Obviously, he was of higher rank than Nicodemus, but Malachi had no idea of his exact position.

"I am interested in your conversation with the Temple guard." The cultured voice was smooth and reassuring. "Word came to me that you are searching for the man Jesus. The miracle worker, some have called him—a term you yourself used, I believe."

"Yes, Rabbi." Malachi was careful to show respect by lowering his eyes and bowing slightly. The man was undoubtedly a priest—a Sadducee, Malachi assumed. "I know Jesus only by what I have heard in passing," he continued. "I've never met him myself."

Somehow Malachi could not bring himself to look his host in the eye, but he was sure that the man must be studying him. There was a long moment of silence.

"Are you on speaking terms with any of this person's friends? his followers, perhaps?"

"No, Rabbi, but I am on a quest to see if what they say about him is true—the miracles, the stories. I understand Jesus of Nazareth is a marvelous storyteller."

"H'mm. The stories, of course, he uses in his teaching among the masses of the illiterate, the poor—and sometimes even with the educated." Malachi's host relaxed and smiled. "And the miracles? Well, as difficult as some of the accounts are to believe, I believe they may be genuine."

Finally Malachi dared to raise his eyes a little. "Then you think that he could possibly be the one for whom all Israel has waited?"

"You're referring to the Messiah?" The man raised his eyebrows. "Well, the common people obviously think so. That display of royalty on the road into Jerusalem yesterday certainly indicates that some of them are convinced. His 'triumphal inaugural ride,' they've been calling it. Most impressive, to be sure." He frowned. "Actually, I'm waiting myself for a few remaining pieces of the puzzle to come together."

"Then you are at least open to the idea that it is possible?" Malachi tried to conceal his excitement.

The official's face became impassive. "He and I have not met privately," he said slowly, cautiously. "I have seen him infrequently—three times in person, I believe."

Malachi waited breathlessly for the priest to continue. Although Malachi had failed to meet Nicodemus, here was someone who could surely give a valid opinion of Jesus of Nazareth, and his rank must be even greater than that of Rabbi Nicodemus.

"You are in search of this man called Jesus?" the priest questioned. "I gather that you would like to speak with him yourself if you had a chance?"

"Perhaps," Malachi replied cautiously, not sure where he stood with his host. Were they to be friends? It didn't seem possible. Religious leaders did not often associate with ordinary people such as Malachi. While Malachi was not a poor man, neither was he one of the elite, and, for all practical purposes, he was still a stranger to this man of prominence in the holy city of Jerusalem.

"At the moment," Malachi said carefully, "I am hoping to learn more about Jesus of Nazareth from those in a position to tell me something about his mission. Already I have spoken with several—I must say I have learned much during these past few days. Yesterday I heard from a man who claimed that Jesus had raised him from the dead. Lazarus of Bethany was his name."

Malachi paused, as if waiting for a response from the Temple official, but then rushed on. He did not notice the other man's frown deepen. "And from what I hear, there were many witnesses at the grave site."

"And do you believe his story?" The priest's voice betrayed no emotion.

"I don't know what I think. Yesterday I thought I might, but today it all seems so outlandish, so utterly impossible, and I'm thinking it can't be true. I'm not sure God operates that way anymore—raising the dead, I mean. Anyway, it's stories like his that I've been tracking down."

The priest stiffened, slowly stroked his beard, and studied Malachi. "And what exactly is it that you wish to know?"

"I wish to know whether he is indeed the one we have waited for so long, someone who will deliver us from the Romans. Someone who will give us back our pride and dignity and our place at the head of the kingdoms of this world." Malachi hoped he sounded sincere. He certainly wanted to be.

"I am impressed with your sincerity and your devotion to this mission." The religious leader seemed to relax. His words were reassuring once again. "You will not be disappointed, I am sure. They say this Jesus of Nazareth is one of the most impressive individuals you would ever chance to meet. I am told he is warm and compassionate in his ministry—personable, even shrewd at times. An amazing combination of qualities, considering his background." A smirk flickered at the corners of his mouth.

Then the Sadducee paused as if remembering something. "I myself have watched him exchange friendly glances with a beggar, and I have seen him speak sternly to the arrogant among us. He is simple but not illiterate, yet undeniably kingly in his bearing, and most certainly one of the best public speakers we have had in Jerusalem recently."

The words had almost a sense of admiration about them, as if that was the only way he could describe Jesus of Nazareth. And yet, strangely enough, Malachi also sensed a patronizing tone.

"I was wondering," the Sadducee now spoke confidentially as though he and Malachi had been friends for years, "when you have found what you are searching for, would you be willing to return to my chambers here and bring me word of where I can find this person called Jesus? I would prefer to meet him in a quiet out-of-the way place so that we do not draw a great deal of public attention. It would never do for us to give the Temple grapevine a chance to do its baleful work." He flashed Malachi an almost impish smile. "For the time being I wish to reserve a degree of anonymity—to keep this encounter as confidential and discrete as possible. You understand, of course?"

Malachi glanced at the face of his host. The merchant was not sure why, but somehow he sensed that the official was now probing him for information. It felt strange. He could understand the rabbi's feeling of caution, but suddenly he knew he would not find the answers he sought in this majestic suite of rooms.

In the distance Malachi could hear the Temple priests chanting their evening hymns. It was a special time of day when worshipers gathered in God's house to pray and recite Scripture. Suddenly he wondered if the tumult still continued in the Temple courtyard. The solitude of these inner chambers seemed to shut them out along with the rest of the world.

Was this sacred place full of God-fearing people who wished for nothing more than to see his name glorified? Were they all searching for truth as Malachi was? Could it be so, or was the whole Temple culture a sham, a charade waiting to be unmasked?

The priest slowly stood, bringing Malachi back to the reality of the moment. "Young man, you never told me your name."

"Oh, I'm sorry. My name is Malachi—Malachi, son of Obed. I'm a merchant from Caesarea, and—peace be to you, Rabbi. Thank you for this opportunity to speak with you." Malachi bowed his head in respect.

His host nodded, and then cleared his throat importantly. "And I am Caiaphas. Shalom, my son. May the God of our fathers Abraham, Isaac, and Jacob bless you, and before many days, may you return to these honored chambers and bring me good news."

Malachi turned to go. The Temple guard who had escorted him to the elegant chambers now returned him to the real world outside. And the nearer Malachi approached the Temple courtyard, the more disturbing the noisy clamor of the Temple marketplace became. It slowly began to overwhelm him like the weight of a giant millstone hung around his neck. Suddenly he wanted to escape this place of spiritual madness and confusion.

Somehow he managed to push his way through the crowd to one of the gates and then hurried down the wide stairs to the streets below the Temple mount. A sense of relief flooded his mind as he wended his way through the milling people, pack animals, and merchandise filling every public area of Jerusalem.

As he rounded a corner, he turned for one last glimpse of the Temple complex, and a strange sight met his eyes. From every opening to the Temple courtyard there exploded frightened people and frantic livestock. They fairly tripped over one another in their haste to escape.

I wonder what all that is about? he mused to himself. *I've never seen so many people move so fast. It's almost as if the place was on fire. That, or someone had decided to clean house.* Malachi wondered whether he should investigate what the commotion was all about, but then decided against it. He had experienced enough chaos for one day.

Chapter Five

TUESDAY

By the time Malachi had reached a city gate, he knew he had made a mistake. The stench of dung and rotting garbage told him so. *Wrong gate,* he chided himself. He couldn't remember ever having used this gate before, and now he knew why. It was obvious that no respectable citizen of Jerusalem ever came here.

The raucous call of a raven grated in Malachi's ears as he stepped through the gate. He knew instantly that the buzzing of flies in the area could mean only one thing—he must be at the gate leading to the Hinnom Valley and the city dump. Where else would one find the constant stench of death itself? Smoldering fires down one gully and then another smelled of burnt chicken feathers and animal bones. Dung lay about in piles, and here and there he could see a vulture picking at the remains of a carcass now covered with maggots. Quickly Malachi spun on his heel to reenter the city.

"Take a wrong turn?"

Malachi swung back in surprise at the sound of the sneering voice. A man in partial armor was sitting under a sycamore tree, sharpening his sword. He ran a whetting stone down the full length of the steel blade before holding it up in the glint of the sun to examine its edge. His unshaven face and unkempt appearance told Malachi that the man belonged to the lower ranks of the Roman army. Perhaps he was one of those barbarian mercenaries brought from the northern reaches of the Empire. Cringing, Malachi knew that he would never want to have to meet this soldier in a dark alley.

"Guess you must be a stranger to the city, or you never would have stumbled this way." The soldier laughed a disdain that sounded for all the world like the cry of the raven sitting above him on the scraggly tree branch. He cleared his throat noisily and spat on the ground in front of him.

As Malachi again wheeled about to escape the stench, he thought he heard a groan. Glancing around and then behind him, he saw a man hanging by leather cords from a whipping post off to one side. Malachi quickly glanced at the soldier sitting under the sycamore tree, then focused on what he figured had to be a prisoner.

It was obvious the man had been hanging by the leather cords for some time—all night, no doubt. The leather had cut into his flesh and his arms had swollen to an ugly purple shade. Malachi grimaced.

The man groaned again, but did not move. Malachi gasped when he noticed the marks of a small whip on the prisoner's shoulders. Welts covered his back and the blows had even flayed loose a few ribbons of flesh. "I shouldn't be here," Malachi muttered to himself as he stared. The man had to be a lawbreaker of some sort, and it wasn't safe to be around when the Romans were dealing with criminals. By the looks of what remained of his garments, Malachi figured the prisoner was a Jew.

Malachi turned toward the Roman soldier again. He knew he had to do something to relieve the man's misery. The suffering he was going through must be excruciating. He could expect little mercy from the Roman soldier keeping guard. "Would it be all right if I gave the prisoner some water?" His words sounded weak and halfhearted.

The soldier ignored Malachi's request, his mind on the piece of fish he had pulled from a leather bag at his side.

"Sir," Malachi knew he was being ignored for a reason, "may I have your permission to help the prisoner just a bit? A drink of water would be enough, I think."

The man in armor glanced at Malachi briefly before turning to stare out over the Valley of Hinnom. It was obvious he was waiting for something—money, no doubt. Malachi shuddered at the thought of having to pay him a bribe. Everything within him recoiled from the idea of giving anything to someone who represented Roman oppression. Then Malachi glanced at the prisoner again. Unfortunately, a bribe would probably be the only thing that would get him permission to aid the prisoner.

Reaching into his belt, Malachi took out a modest coin. He walked toward the soldier with an outstretched hand, but the soldier ignored it. Only after Malachi pulled out a second coin and extended it also to the soldier did the mercenary show any sort of recognition. He took the coins and gestured toward a waterskin hanging from a nearby tree branch.

The day was heating up—already the sun was halfway up the eastern horizon. Malachi squinted at the glaring ball of fire in the sky. By now he had hoped to be on his way to the small town of Bethlehem on business. If he hurried, even now he could travel the five miles there and back before nightfall.

Pulling a cup from the folds of his cloak, Malachi poured a drink for the prisoner hanging at the ends of the leather thongs. He tipped the cup to the man's lips in hopes that the water would rouse him.

The prisoner groaned again and opened his eyes. He accepted the rest of the water from the cup and then tried to stand, only to wince in pain. Not until then did Malachi notice the lacerated flesh hanging from the sides and bottoms of his bare feet. Evidently the prisoner's feet had also been beaten to prevent him from attempting to escape.

"What is your name?" Malachi gently asked.

The man stared at Malachi through glazed eyes. It was obvious he was not altogether coherent yet, as he frowned and then took a deep breath but did not answer.

"How long have you been here?"

The man licked his swollen parched lips and blinked several times. "I'm not sure. Since yesterday about noon, I think. What day is it?"

"The third day of the week. Is there something else you need? May I get you some food?"

"Yes, that would be good. A little bread, or fish if you have some."

Malachi pulled yet another item from the folds of his garments—a chunk of bread. After spending years on the road, he knew just what to take on a journey.

The prisoner ate the bread gratefully, though he couldn't even feed himself. He savored every morsel, and when he finished, he gave a contented sort of sigh.

"Tell me," Malachi kept on, "how did you end up here?"

The prisoner looked at Malachi and then tilted his head back in despair. "Oh, the usual, I guess." He sighed. "I was part of a gang of thieves down on the Jericho road. For five years we worked out of caves on that deserted stretch of road just before it reaches the Jordan Valley. No one could ever catch us." The prisoner stretched to get the circulation in his arms going again, but flinched as the pain from the soles of his feet forced him to stand on his toes.

"Unfortunately, they laid an ambush for us. Day before yesterday." He nodded toward the soldier half dozing in the shade of the sycamore.

"We should have known it was a trap," he groaned. "It was too easy. The merchants in that caravan didn't even have an escort, but we had been used to doing what we wanted for so long that we never saw it coming. The soldiers killed some of my companions. I would have been killed, too, if I hadn't surrendered." The prisoner shook his head in despair. "I only wish I had fought to the death like the others. I don't know what I was thinking! I was just a coward, I guess."

Malachi said nothing. There was not much he could say. The penalty for thievery was severe—and inevitable.

The prisoner stretched his wrists again to bring back a tingling sensation to his arms. "Tell me," he asked, "why did you do it? Why did you stop to give me a drink of water? That was a dangerous thing to do, you know."

"I know," Malachi sighed. "I am quite aware of the danger here, but I wouldn't feel right about doing nothing—and besides, money talks." He lowered his voice and nodded toward the soldier in the shade. "Especially to one like him."

"Well, it was kind of you. I'm truly grateful." The prisoner changed the subject. "Do you live in Jerusalem?"

"No, I come from Caesarea, on the coast. I'm here on business—I trade in fine carpets." Malachi realized that anything he said was meaningless to the man's plight. He searched the prisoner's face. "So what will you do now?"

As soon as he said it Malachi wished he hadn't. Everyone knew of the contempt the Romans had toward Jewish prisoners.

And their fellow Jews cared little more. The Jewish leaders—at least the Pharisees—consigned a condemned person to damnation.

There was no hope or salvation for such an individual. No redemption. No forgiveness or atonement possible.

The prisoner's shoulders sagged, and he trembled from pain.

"What I mean," Malachi added, "is, have you made your peace with God?"

The prisoner stared at him through unfocused eyes and took a deep breath again. "My mother died when I was 4, and then a fever took my father. What little family I had left could not feed another mouth, and my uncle sold me as a slave to a caravan leader. Eventually I found day work on a small farm. But that family could not afford me either, especially after they lost their land after a drought. That's when I joined a group of bandits fighting to overthrow both the Romans and our own wealthy oppressors. We've spent our time plundering the wealthy and raiding Roman garrisons. As I said before, no one could catch us."

The prisoner shifted his weight again. "Eventually I got pretty tired of always being on the run, you know. Once I thought life was going to take a turn for the better, but things didn't work out."

"A turn for the better?" Malachi ventured.

"Well, it seemed so at the time. I went to hear that new teacher, Jesus of Nazareth." The prisoner's eyes lighted up a bit. "It was amazing! He stirred my soul as no one ever had. I knew in my heart that what he had to offer was exactly what I needed—hope and a decent cause to live for. Jesus could heal people of any disease. You name it—if they had it, he could cure it. So I figured he had to be the Messiah and would free our people from the Romans. It made me feel different somehow. Not that I changed my lifestyle much—I still belonged to the bandit gang, but I felt different."

"Different?"

"Yeah, different—as though I wanted to be a better person."

The prisoner tried to straighten his shoulders and then groaned. He took a deep breath. "I remember one time we were planning to rob a merchant caravan that we knew would take the Jericho road in the morning. It was the first day of the week—I still remember it clearly. At any rate, the caravan didn't come by on schedule, so we were getting pretty restless. Barabbas said we should just cancel the attack, because the whole thing might be a trap. He was the leader, a real revolutionary.

"A few minutes later an unsuspecting traveler on the road wandered by. He looked like he might be carrying money, so a couple of the men attacked him and beat him. They stripped him of everything he had—even his clothes.

"We didn't wait around much for fear of getting caught, but later that day my friend Amos and I were posted as a lookout. We saw two men traveling the road. First came a priest—he looked as if he was in a hurry. Could we blame him? He took one look at the man we had robbed and just hurried on—didn't even stop to help the poor man. Then a Levite went by and didn't stop either. We let the priest and the Levite go on since, as revolutionaries, we usually plundered only the landowners and Romans."

The prisoner paused and painfully shifted his weight from one foot to the other again. He looked at Malachi, and a puzzled expression crossed his face. "And then a third man appeared with his donkey. A donkey would be a worthwhile prize, you know. Anyway, he slowed down when he saw the man we had beaten lying beside the road. Not even looking around to see if there was any danger, he just got down off his donkey, took care of the poor man's wounds, then put him on his donkey and went on his way.

"Amos wanted to rob him, but I wouldn't let him. The man's act of kindness impressed me and made me feel the way I did when I was with Jesus. And the man with the donkey was a Samaritan! As much as I had always hated Samaritans, I had to respect him. A Samaritan helping a Jew—I had never seen anything like it!"

The thief paused to catch his breath. For several minutes he remained silent. Finally he raised his eyes to Malachi and said slowly, "But as you see, though I thought I had changed, it just wasn't enough. The life of a bandit was the only one I knew.

"And as I said, a few days later the Romans ambushed us. Five or six of us died, and I think four escaped into the hills. The Romans captured Barabbas, Amos, and me. Amos was my best friend. That's him over there on that dung heap with Barabbas. The Roman soldiers beat them both unconscious, but I think they're probably still alive."

For the first time Malachi noticed the two bodies in a gully half-filled with animal dung. He shuddered, but his thoughts were still on the thief's story. Here was a man who had met Jesus and had the chance to accept Jesus and follow him, but had not taken the opportunity. Why?

Once again the prisoner shifted his weight from one foot to the other and took several shuddering gasps of air. Malachi knew there was nothing more he could do to ease the prisoner's terrible pain, except give him a little more water, perhaps. The prisoner gulped down the water gratefully and then began to talk again.

"One day I was in the Temple," he continued, "about this time last year. The priests and rabbis were having a public forum in the Temple court to answer questions about Jesus of Nazareth. Until then I thought I had him pretty much figured out, but they said some things that I really couldn't contradict. I couldn't prove them wrong, not that I'm smart or anything."

"Such as?"

"His being poor and all. He came from Nazareth. 'Can anything good come out of Nazareth?' That's the line the priests kept using." The prisoner caught his breath and suddenly groaned as though seized by a fresh wave of pain. Gritting his teeth, he had to wait a minute before he could continue.

"And then there's the fact that he doesn't teach like the leaders of our nation. He claims that he is speaking only truth, but the rabbis claim that it's not possible for just one person to be right and all the other leaders to be wrong. Anyway, that's what they said, and I figured they must be right. It didn't make sense that a poor man could be the Messiah, so I was sure he had to be a fraud."

"But what about the miracles everyone talks about?"

"Oh, that—well, every rabbi I talked to said it was probably demons working through him. Demons can work miracles too, you know."

"So you gave up on the idea of his being the Messiah?"

"Why wouldn't I?" the prisoner said bitterly. His speech came slower now. "But then I don't know what I think anymore." He sighed. "And what's the use anyway? I'm too evil to be saved." The prisoner sighed, and his shoulders slumped. He again began to groan loudly as he had to force himself to stand on both bleeding feet."

The Roman guard jerked awake from his nap in the shade and sat up. He glared at Malachi and then the prisoner.

"Just a couple more minutes," Malachi promised, patting his leather money pouch reassuringly.

The guard reached for a flask of wine setting by his side. After taking a few swigs, he leaned back against the tree trunk with a grunt.

"Could I have another drink of water?" the prisoner begged.

Malachi poured him some more water, then asked, "So I guess you aren't ready to die?"

The prisoner hung his head again. "While there is life, there is still hope," he mumbled, "but no, I guess I'm not. I just wish—I wish there was some way I could make up for all the wrongs I've done. If I could just relive a few days of my life, then I could—" The man's voice choked, and Malachi found himself swallowing hard to keep his own feelings under control.

Like the others that Malachi had spoken to—Simon of Bethany, Lazarus, Caiaphas—this man had a story to tell, but his was different. No longer could the prisoner debate whether Jesus was a genuine miracle worker sent from God even if his teachings did challenge Jewish traditions. Life would soon be over for the thief now hanging from a whipping post.

With pity in his eyes, Malachi asked, "So what happens next?"

The prisoner's voice was dull and empty of emotion. "Oh, they'll probably take the three of us to the place of execution on the public road beyond the Damascus gate—and crucify us."

"When?"

The Roman guard stirred. "Probably by the end of the week!" he sneered, then roared with delight. "Friday, if we're lucky." He stiffly climbed to his feet. Pointing to Malachi, he announced, "You need to be moving along now! You've had enough time with the criminal."

Bitterly aware that there was nothing that he could do now, Malachi turned to the thief now once more slumped at the ends of the leather cords. "Don't give up hope," Malachi whispered.

"Maybe there is something to this Jesus of Nazareth. I've heard he heals both broken bodies and broken hearts." The prisoner did not reply.

Malachi tossed the guard another coin as he headed back toward the city gate. Three prisoners to be crucified—and quickly forgotten.

Chapter Six

WEDNESDAY

It was still early morning when Malachi started down the street in front of the inn. Stretching in an attempt to wake himself up, he shoved the last bite of bread into his mouth and sighed. What should he do now? He had spent the previous day just getting to Bethlehem to speak to an influential merchant interested in Malachi's carpets. Malachi already had quite a stock of carpets in Jerusalem, so he had arranged to meet the merchant to discuss arrangements.

But the unexpected encounter with the thief in the Valley of Hinnom had delayed him, and then he hadn't arrived in Bethlehem until noon, when the merchants shut their shops and stalls for a couple hours. Not until midafternoon did Malachi finally locate the merchant's shop. It had taken more time than he had wanted—but business was business.

It was always that way. Business contacts were important, but he couldn't help wondering what was really most important in his life right now. Was it his business? his wife and children? Rachel was a wonderful wife, and he wished that he did not have to spend so much time away from home.

Or was his search for the Messiah even more vital? Malachi knew that more than anything he wanted to find Jesus and really settle in his mind whether Jesus of Nazareth was the Messiah. The question seemed to occupy his every waking thought.

Today, his business appointment completed, Malachi was free to continue his search for the truth about Jesus. Again he decided he would start at the Temple. Despite its noise and confusion, it was still the center of Jerusalem's religious life. Surely someone there would have the answers to his questions. He would just have to avoid the parts of the Temple that disturbed him.

Anyway, Malachi just knew he couldn't leave Jerusalem until he had spent at least one more day in the Temple. Maybe he would even encounter Jesus there, hear him preach, or even see him work some of his famed miracles.

By now, Malachi knew that he wanted to meet Jesus more than anything. After all, he had heard reports about him from an innkeeper, Rabbi Simon, Lazarus of Bethany, the high priest, and the thief in the Valley of Hinnom. Malachi knew he couldn't deny it any longer—Jesus must indeed be the longawaited One.

But from the beginning Malachi had also resolved to be cautious. Others had claimed to be messiahs, only to lead their followers into disaster. Simon, a royal servant, and Athonges had claimed to be messiahs after the death of Herod, only to lead their followers to destruction by the Romans. If Malachi finally did meet Jesus and accept him, he wanted to do it on his own terms. No sensationalism or revolutionary frenzy.

As Malachi took a deep breath of morning air, he let the shafts of sunlight penetrating between the buildings bathe his face with their pleasant warmth. Even at this hour the streets were crowded. Young girls returning from the city wells wended their way down the narrow streets, and gangling herd boys goaded their unruly flocks of goats and sheep to the city marketplace. Already old men were sitting together to warm themselves in the morning sunshine and play board games to while away the hours.

But the Temple grounds were still relatively uncrowded when Malachi entered through the Beautiful Gate. The Temple vendors were preparing for the day. Up went the colorful awnings to block out the sun. Out came the tables of the money changers. A fat merchant with dangling gold earrings sat against the courtyard wall, busily counting out stacks of coins and placing them on a low table in front of him. He had copper ones, and silver, and even some gold ones. A small toddler wandered too close to the little stacks of coins, but an angry scowl from the merchant sent the child back to the folds of his mother's garments.

Malachi ambled on through the wide outer courtyard. He realized that it was probably the first real break he had taken since the previous Sabbath to just enjoy himself in the holy city of Jerusalem.

So much history. So many stories and traditions. The religious heritage of it all fairly made his head swim. Malachi was proud of everything the city stood for.

He passed into the Court of the Women and chose a stone bench along the wall of the inner court so that he could sit and rest and plan. It was one of the busiest spots in the whole Temple. Everyone came here—men, women, and children. Here everyone brought their offerings and placed them in the trumpet-shaped contribution boxes—some out of a sense of duty, perhaps, to help with the upkeep of the place. Others, no doubt, came to parade their wealth.

Malachi settled himself back a little farther on the bench. It was a blessing to bring an offering to the house of God—to listen to the glorious chants of praise by the Levite singers—to worship. Yet, in spite of the sacredness of the place, it appeared that people had still other reasons for being there too. Women came and went in groups, giggling and chattering quietly among themselves. Malachi noticed men standing in out-of-the-way places stroking their beards, and he wondered if they were discussing their latest business deals. The way their voices rose and fell with laughter on the early-morning air convinced him that that must be what they were doing.

For some, being at the Temple was just part of their job. A cleaning woman worked her way across the stone pavement, sweeping in short, circular strokes. As Malachi watched the stooped shoulders doing the thankless task, he decided that she must have experienced much of what went on in the Temple, at least in the two outer courts. No doubt, she had probably heard Jesus teach in the Temple court, or had even seen his miracles. Malachi could ask her about Jesus. Because she worked in the public areas of the Temple she would probably feel less intimidated at the thought of talking to a stranger. At least it was worth a try.

"Excuse me, good woman, may I speak with you a moment?"

The woman did not respond at first. She went right on sweeping, engrossed in her task. However, as the arcs of the broom brought her nearer to the place where Malachi was sitting, he tried again.

"Good woman, could I trouble you for a moment of your time?"

Pausing, the woman turned to face him.

"I was wondering." Malachi chose his words carefully. "Have you seen Jesus of Nazareth, the miracle worker, lately? Has he been here in Jerusalem, maybe to teach here in the Temple?"

The woman glanced at the passersby momentarily, and then back at Malachi. "Yes, he has been here," she responded in a timid voice. "He was here just yesterday."

Malachi's pulse quickened as he realized that soon he was going to come face to face with Israel's Messiah. Excitement surged through him as he studied the woman's face, eager for more details, but she simply stood waiting for him to continue.

"Did he speak here? Did he perform some miracles?"

The woman stepped a little closer to Malachi to clear the way for the Temple traffic trying to pass. "I didn't see him perform any miracles. Not here. He was teaching during the morning, and then the scribes and priests began asking him questions." Her voice was even and steady, but Malachi sensed an undercurrent in her tone.

"Things got pretty exciting for a while, when the chief scribe, Rabbi Phineas, began to challenge Jesus. Rabbi Phineas acted as if he was just wanting to have a theological discussion, but I think a lot of onlookers knew that he was trying to trick Jesus into saying something wrong. I could tell, but then"—she looked around her and lowered her voice—"I think many of these religious leaders are more concerned about their popularity than how they can honor God."

Malachi smiled at the woman's statement. "So things got exciting, did they? Were they shouting at each other?"

"They were raising their voices—the priests, I mean. Rabbi Phineas kept calm, but at one point two of the chief priests began to shout."

"And what about Jesus?"

"Jesus? He just spoke as though he knew exactly what they were going to say even before they opened their mouth. It was very strange. Almost as if he could read their minds."

Malachi wished that he could have witnessed the encounter. "So what were all the arguments about?"

"Well, they talked about taxes, and marriage, and—the commandments, I think."

Malachi chuckled softly to himself, commenting, "That certainly was a strange combination of topics to discuss."

She smiled. "Yes, I suppose it was, but then, as I said, the priests were trying to start arguments so that they could trap Jesus into saying something that would make him look foolish. Splitting hairs, if you ask me."

"And you heard all this while sweeping?"

The woman blushed and began to pull a shawl up over her chin, but Malachi quickly apologized. "I'm sorry. I was only teasing." He shook his head in embarrassment. "Do you think Jesus will return to the Temple today?"

The woman folded her hands in front of her, then glanced self-consciously at the worshipers passing by. "No, I don't think he will come back today. In fact, I don't think he will come back again at all." She sounded relieved, but a bit disappointed.

"Why not?" Malachi asked in surprise.

"Well, when the scribes and Pharisees and all the priests had nearly worn themselves out, Jesus began to say some pretty serious things—not that they weren't true, but I just never heard anyone ever get up the courage to say the things he did right to their faces. It was kind of frightening."

Malachi felt a keen sense of disappointment that he had missed the encounter. He wished that he could have been there. And to think that he had been so close! "So he bested them, did he?"

The woman smiled sheepishly. "He did at that. I couldn't hear it all, because they were up in the Court of Israel, but I saw and heard enough. When Jesus is here, he usually sits while teaching, but this time he stood." She pointed up through the large gate to the high colonnade of the inner Temple complex. "He walked back and forth among those pillars, and every eye followed him. He called the scribes and Pharisees hypocrites, and he accused them of extortion and fraud in the way they use Temple money. Then he referred to them as blind spiritual guides and fools, and he said that even though they claim to be holy in the way they pray and give tithes and offerings, they are actually mean and cruel and heartless, because they don't mind taking from the poor to give to the rich."

Emotion flashed in the woman's eyes as if she was reliving the moment. "And Jesus just kept on and on—nothing could stop him!" Her words burst from her like a torrent of water. "It was as if he thought he would never again have another chance to say what he needed to say, so he said it all at once. He said the Pharisees and scribes are just like our forefathers who murdered the prophets of God. And then he said they are like the tombs that hold the dead prophets bones—all whitewashed and pretty outside, but inside defiled and hiding the truth about their real spiritual condition."

The woman took a deep breath and became thoughtful. She lowered her voice almost to a whisper. "And then he said, 'Oh, Jerusalem, I have loved you as a mother hen loves her little chicks. You could come to me and be safe under my wings, but you have refused my offer of love and salvation.'"

Malachi knew he needed to let the woman return to her sweeping, but she seemed unwilling to go. "Tell me," he said, "how is it that you work here at the Temple complex? Is your husband a Levite here?"

She lowered her eyes and stared at the stone pavement.

"I'm sorry; did I say the wrong thing?"

"Oh no, it's just that usually no one ever listens to me or seems to care anymore. My husband, God rest his soul, has been gone eight years."

Malachi felt awkward, but the sweeper woman seemed to want to continue.

"When my husband grew ill, my son became afraid that we would have to sell the house to pay our bills, so he came to the priests with the deed to our land and signed everything over to them as a corban Temple gift." She sighed. "And now I have no place to live."

Malachi was indignant. Corban was a way some used to avoid God's command that they use their land or wealth to support their aging parents. By giving their property as a gift to God they could still use it until they died without having to spend it on the elderly. Nothing could shame and dishonor a parent more than a son who refused to care for them. And to refuse to allow the mother to remain in her own home was even worse. "I know of the practice," the merchant said, "but I can't understand why the authorities allow it. My uncle once gave a corban gift, and the rest of the family despised him for it. His mother never did forgive him."

The cleaning woman seemed resigned to her fate. "I never did believe my son's assurances that he would look after me. Anyway, I don't see how it matters much now. At least the priests said they would allow me to stay in one of the storage rooms here at the Temple, but—it's not like home." Her voice trailed off. He knew he shouldn't press the issue further.

But the sweeper woman wasn't finished yet. "Now, Jesus of Nazareth? Any parent would be honored to have him as a son." She picked the broom up from off the floor and pointed with it to one of the trumpet-shaped offering containers. "I'll never forget the day he came here and sat right there beside that offering box. He and his disciples were here, and I was here in the woman's court with my friend Miriam, finishing up my sweeping for the day. She is a widow. It was late afternoon, and she had her offering with her. It was the preparation day, and she always tries to give something as a thank offering on the preparation day.

"Miriam was afraid that Jesus and his disciples might see her give her offering because it was such a small pittance. She waited for them to leave, but they stayed and stayed. Finally when Jesus was talking to his disciples, she slipped her coins into the offering box, hoping he would not see her. One of the coins got lost in the folds of her shawl, and as she fumbled with it, I could see the men watching her. I know that Miriam was embarrassed." The sweeper woman hesitated. "I don't know why I'm telling you all this."

"Go on," he encouraged her.

She paused, and then finally added, "You see, Miriam had only two mites, the smallest coins possible—but it was everything she possessed."

The woman shook her head. "Other people were dropping in large gifts—some whole bags of money. Later Miriam told me how badly she felt that she was giving so little compared to others, but do you know, Jesus saw her drop those two tiny coins into the box. I'm sure he did, because I heard him say so to his disciples. He said that God would bless Miriam, because she had put in more than all the others, those who did not have to sacrifice anything to give. I just couldn't believe it! He said that about my friend Miriam!" Tears trickled down the woman's cheeks now, and she didn't even try to wipe them away.

Chapter Seven

THURSDAY

Little clouds of dust puffed around Malachi's sandaled feet as he trudged the road eastward out of Jerusalem. Red and yellow poppies, mallows, chamomile, aenmones, and wildflowers carpeted the land, and here and there a sycamore fig tree hugged the narrow road. Olive orchards and vineyards blanketed the terraces and valleys, stretching down and away from Jerusalem, and toward Bethlehem, Malachi could see the ripening barley fields.

Malachi mopped the back of his neck with his handkerchief. If the dust hadn't been so annoying, he would have felt more like enjoying the view. Another day nearly spent, and still Malachi had not seen Jesus or heard of his whereabouts. By now, more than anything else, he longed to see the miracle worker from Galilee.

Unfortunately, Jesus had remained fairly illusive after his run-in with the Temple aristocrats. That had been two days ago. No one seemed to know where he had gone. After the encounter with the priests and scribes in the Temple, it seemed that Jesus had literally disappeared into thin air. Everyone knew that the House of God was his favorite place to come, but now it almost appeared as though Jesus had abandoned the Temple to the feuding Pharisees and Sadducees.

The innkeeper was Malachi's resident authority on the location of anybody and everybody that a merchant might need to contact for business purposes. And the innkeeper had given him some pretty good tips on those who might know about Jesus. Yesterday he had advised Malachi to visit Bethany again, since that was where Jesus spent much of his time when he was in Judea.

Malachi felt angry with himself for having walked away from a perfectly good opportunity to meet Jesus at Rabbi Simon's feast. Of course, Malachi hadn't really been on the guest list for the feast in spite of the rabbi's invitation, and he had had a business appointment. Business! Always business got in the way of the really important things in life! Why hadn't he stayed to meet Jesus? He wondered now with a certain sense of foreboding if he might regret even more that decision in the future.

And then yesterday afternoon it would certainly have fit in with Malachi's plans to go to Bethany as the innkeeper had advised, but unfortunately, a kinsman and his family had showed up. Their visit occupied the rest of the afternoon.

And then this morning the innkeeper's boy had suddenly become sick. In exchange for a free night's lodging, Malachi had agreed to search of a physician. What he had expected would take an hour at the most, had consumed half the day. Malachi hadn't thought that finding a good doctor in Jerusalem would be so difficult, but then it was Passover and the demand for medical help had to be high. Thousands of people had already arrived for the Passover festivities, and before the weekend, thousands more would be showing up.

The first doctor's fee would have been exorbitant, and the second doctor wouldn't come to the inn to examine the boy. Said he was too busy, even at the price Malachi offered him. Malachi had needed to find a third one, and then he had to search the shops and markets for the right herbs and other ingredients for the physician's treatment. By the time he had finished the task Malachi was frustrated and disgusted. It was yet another example of the wealthy getting even richer at the expense of the common people. And it made him appreciate his own health, and that of his family.

What a shame, he thought, *that Jesus, the healer, was not somewhere in the area.* Supposedly he could cure any sickness or ailment, yet the innkeeper seemed oblivious to the fact—or unbelieving.

Well, yesterday—and everything since then—seemed a lifetime ago. Now Malachi was finally on his way to Bethany. The little town was not quite two miles away. He could have saddled his donkey and ridden the distance, but he had lent the donkey to the innkeeper's wife for another free night's lodging. She needed a beast of burden to help in her preparations for the Passover. Besides all her responsibilities at the inn, she was helping with the Passover meal for a large family gathering across town. No matter; the walk would do him good.

As he followed the path up and over the Mount of Olives, Malachi realized that most of the traffic was coming his way. He kept to the edge of the road until the number of incoming pilgrims began to thin out. It wasn't until he had passed the summit that he realized someone was following closely behind him. Vaguely he wondered why the man did not pass.

Finally he ventured a greeting. "Shalom, my friend! What takes you out of Jerusalem on the eve of Passover?"

"Ah yes, the Passover." The stranger pulled alongside of Malachi. "This is my first Passover in Jerusalem, and what an adventure it is."

"You're from Galilee?"

"Yes. How did you know?"

"Your accent betrays you, my friend." The two laughed together as though they were old friends.

"I know this weekend will be a time of great rejoicing for me and for all Jerusalem," the stranger announced, "but today I am in search of something even more important."

"More important?" Malachi raised his eyebrows in surprise. What could be greater than the Passover celebration?

"I am looking for an old friend of mine," the other man said. "I have heard that he sometimes visits the small village of Bethany not far from here, so I am going there this afternoon to see if I can find him."

"So am I." Malachi was intrigued by their common goals. "I mean, I'm also looking for someone in Bethany. His name is Jesus of Nazareth."

The man stared at him in surprise. "Jesus of Nazareth? The miracle worker from Galilee? That's who I'm looking for!" The Galilean stopped in the middle of the road and took Malachi by the shoulder. "So you know where I can find him!"

"Actually, no. But I have been told he stays at the home of Lazarus, the man everyone says he raised from the dead."

"He raised a man from the dead!" The stranger had a dumbfounded expression on his face, as if he were hearing too much good news for one day. "This is incredible, my friend, but I guess I shouldn't be surprised. I must meet this Lazarus. Like me, he has been blessed by God."

He extended his hand. "My name is Silas. You have given me much to look forward to tonight. I am grateful for life, and a clear mind, and God's gift of grace for one like me." Silas paused and then hurried on in explanation.

"Without a doubt, meeting Jesus has been the most incredible thing that has ever happened to me—he has been the difference between life and death. When he looked at me that first time and spoke my name, he sent shivers running down my spine. His is truly the voice of God speaking through the Son of Man."

Malachi studied the stranger. "I've heard others say so," he agreed. "Lazarus, and Simon the Pharisee—both have been touched by the healing hand of Jesus."

"Before I met Jesus, My life was in shambles, but it wasn't always so." Silas seemed to be driven by an urge to tell his story. He and Malachi had to step to the side of a narrow bend in the roadway to allow a group of pilgrims to pass. "My father was the local magistrate in our town—in the Gentile territories east of the Sea of Tiberius—so my family had a comfortable life. As children, my brother and I pretty much got whatever we wanted."

"But at the same we dabbled in magic and sorcery." Silas blinked hard. "And then we tried necromancy."

He squinted against the bright sunlight of the afternoon as he continued. "I became so involved that I even began talking to the spirits myself. At first my friends and I had always gone through a medium, but one night someone urged me to contact the spirits myself. I gave it a try—and became trapped. The sense of power was like wine to a drunkard, and it scared me. I tried to escape the whole nightmare, but it had me in its grip. And then when my fellow demon worshipers began to talk about a human sacrifice, I knew I had to get out!

"It wasn't until we actually went through with a ritual in which we had to sacrifice a human life that I knew I was finished with the occult. And I told my friends so. I said that I was leaving, but they said I couldn't. That we were all in this thing too deep.

"But I insisted, and when they tried to stop me, something snapped inside of me at that moment. I began to lash out at all of them like a wild beast—like a madman."

The stranger paused and looked at Malachi intently. "I know what I'm telling you here today sounds terrible, but it's true—every word of it." He put his hand to his head. "And if it hadn't been for Jesus, I would be dead in some cold dark grave somewhere."

Malachi wondered if he should be on the road with a total stranger who had such a terrible past. Fortunately, it wasn't far to Bethany now.

Silas noticed Malachi's uneasy expression and stopped by the side of the road. "I'm sorry," he stammered. "I've said too much. I—I shouldn't have bothered you with all this, but I only told you because I'm so excited at the transformation Jesus has made in my life. I—" He stopped and looked at Malachi as if he didn't expect him to believe his story.

Malachi hesitated only an instant. "No, it's all right. I believe you; it's just that—as a Jew, I have been raised to despise people who worship the devil and serve his evil demons. I can see that Jesus has made a wonderful change in your life." After a pause Malachi hurried on. "Go ahead, finish your story."

Silas took a deep breath as they began walking again. "Well, when my friends grabbed me, I became a wild beast. As some of them tried to hold me down, I began screaming and clawing at them. One grabbed a club to defend himself, and I turned on him. I snatched the club right out of his hand and began to hit him with it. I beat him and kept on beating him. I beat him senseless—and I killed him." The stranger's voice was subdued. "He was one of my best friends, and I killed him."

For a moment Silas said nothing, head down as they walked along, his face mirroring the horror and grief of the memories. Malachi suddenly sensed how difficult it must be to speak of such an experience. If it had been him, would he tell others what had happened to him as Silas was doing, or would he always keep it a dark secret?

"When I calmed down later that night," Silas continued after he had regained control of himself, "they took me away and locked me up in a dungeon. They bound me in chains and brought me out only to hear my case before the magistrate. My father couldn't take the case because I was his relative, so they brought an official in from Gamala, and he sentenced me to be executed.

"And then it happened again. It was the second time I remember losing control of myself and going berserk. A superhuman power just seemed to take control of my body. I snapped the chains off the manacles that held my wrists together, and broke the leg irons from off my ankles. After that, everything became a blur—until I met Jesus."

"If Jesus can do that for you," Malachi said after a long silence, "he must really be an amazing person!"

Silas nodded reverently. "He's more than amazing. He's the Son of God."

Suddenly the two men realized that they had reached Bethany. They stopped a man passing by with a lamb in his arms and asked him if he knew whether Jesus had been to the village that day. The man did not know, but he pointed them to the home of Lazarus. Jesus was not there, and with a sickening feeling in the pit of his stomach, Malachi knew that he had missed him again. Would he never catch up with the miracle worker from Galilee?

"The hour is late. Won't you stay and celebrate the Passover," Lazarus and his sisters asked Malachi and Silas. "You have no place else to go, and we would be honored to share the evening with two fellow believers."

Malachi spent the evening with the others eating the Passover meal. Then as he and Silas spread their mats in the small courtyard garden out under the stars, Malachi asked the former demoniac to finish telling his experience. "So you met Jesus. Where did this happen, and how?"

"Oh, it's been more than a year ago, now, I guess," Silas yawned in a sleepy voice. "It was a dreary morning—I'll never forget it. It had rained the night before. Quite a storm, I guess, from what they told us later. At that time, another lunatic and I had been living in the burial caves along the bluffs by the Sea of Galilee. We were so insane that no one would come near us."

Silas's voice grew solemn again, and he spoke reverently. "My first recollection of that morning was that suddenly I was looking into the kindest, most loving God-filled face that I had ever seen. And my mind was clear as a bright morning in the month of Sivan. If it wasn't so serious, I'd laugh, even now." He smiled to himself in the dark. "I was wearing only rags, and by the looks on the faces of Jesus' disciples, we must have really frightened them."

The Gentile lapsed into silence as the night creatures droned out their evening dirges and the wind rustled the Kermes oak trees overhanging the courtyard wall. "I just have one word of advice for you, Malachi," he added sleepily. "Don't wait too long to accept him as your Lord and Master. I knew nothing of him, yet he came to me. And now, Malachi, you have the invitation too. The Spirit of God is tugging at your heart. You don't have to be with him to open your life to him. Just do it here, tonight. Now is the day of salvation for you."

He spoke with such conviction that Malachi felt as if all creation were holding its breath to listen to his response. But was he ready and willing?

Chapter Eight

FRIDAY

The sun burned down on his back as Malachi turned the street corner at Jericho's western gate. The stone pavement radiated spring warmth. Although the full heat of summer had not yet arrived in the City of Palm Trees, the broiling sun in the confines of the narrow Jericho street always took its toll. Sweat trickled down sun-bronzed faces, leaving streaks in the dust kicked up by feet and the wind. Little gray lizards skittered across the stone pavement of the busy thoroughfare.

Malachi paused to mop his perspiring forehead before ducking under a roll of cloth hoisted onto the shoulder of a passing vendor. He sidestepped a camel loaded high with market goods, stumbled over a basket of vegetables in his pathway, and then hastily clutched at the doorpost of a merchant's stall. It was the only way to avoid being pushed aside by a squadron of Roman soldiers on their way to somewhere.

After straightening his head cloth, Malachi brushed away a strand of straw clinging to his tunic. He surveyed the faces of those milling about him at the city gate. A crippled man sitting on the pavement rasped in a husky voice, "Alms for the lame! Alms for the lame!" Little children played tag around Malachi's feet, and a vendor wove his way about among the crowd with a basket of exotic fruits on his head.

The vendor looked exhausted. Come to think of it, Malachi was tired himself. He had left Bethany before the first rays of daylight had pierced the morning air. It had been a long trip down from Jerusalem with the caravan that traveled that way twice daily.

Lazarus had invited Malachi to return again that night to spend the weekend with them in Bethany. "Jesus should be back by then," his host had speculated. "He looked tired yesterday when he and his disciples left here before noon—said he needed some quiet time with them before the evening Passover meal they were planning to share together in Jerusalem."

But Jesus had not yet returned. Lazarus had shared his real concerns with Malachi when his sisters, Mary and Martha, weren't around. "If you ask me, I think there's trouble brewing for the Master. I wish Jesus wouldn't go up to Jerusalem at all until after the weekend."

But Jesus had gone, and now Malachi had business to tend to, and if things worked out, they would all be back in Bethany that night to begin the Sabbath together. It looked as if Malachi was finally going to get to meet Jesus.

Malachi's stomach growled as he stood in the marketplace. Pulling a small copper coin from the folds of his robe, he handed it to the street vendor with the basket of fruit on his head. The tired vendor didn't even haggle at the offering. He merely reached up into the basket perched precariously on his head and removed a pomegranate. Malachi struck the piece of fruit against the mud brick wall beside him to break it open. As he walked along, sucking on one of the myriad seeds in the fruit, he thought of the story the innkeeper had told him the previous day. It was an amazing story—if it was true. If not, it was at least unique.

Malachi scanned the shops and booths in the open square near the northern gate, then stepped up to one of the tables in the busiest part of the square. "I'm looking for the commissioner of finance for the governor," he announced. "Can you tell me where I will find him?"

A gray-bearded man behind the table sat counting stacks of coins in front of him and only briefly glanced at Malachi. "And you would be?" he demanded. The man wore an embroidered waistcoat, a garment reserved only for the rich.

"I'm Malachi, son of Obed, a merchant here on business, looking to find an agent who can begin selling my line of carpets and tapestries. I'm from Caesarea on the coast."

"I know where Caesarea is!" the man snapped impatiently. "Do you think that we here in the Jordan Valley are a bunch of ignorant hicks? We do get out of this place now and then, and I, personally, have been to Caesarea! I'll have you know that my father was a financial advisor in Herod's court."

"I'm sure His Majesty was honored," Malachi hastened to add politely. He pulled two silver coins from his leather purse and handed them to the offended man. "If you would be so kind as to tell me where I might find the commissioner, I would be eternally grateful, and then I would be on my way."

"He's not here this afternoon. Can't say why." The middle-aged man was at least making a pretense at being helpful, if not friendly. "You'll probably find him at his residence," he added. "This boy here will take you to the address." With a wave of his hand he sent Malachi on his way.

Some minutes later Malachi found himself at the gate of the home of someone who was obviously a prominent citizen. The size of the gate told the whole story. Most household gates were just large enough for a man of average height to enter—this one was fully five cubits high.

He called out a greeting of peace to those inside, and then slipped a coin into the hand of the young boy who stood at his side waiting for a gift. If Malachi was lucky, the commissioner should still be home.

When a girl's face appeared at the small window in the gate, Malachi wasn't surprised at the message. "The master of the house is out," she announced. By now Malachi was used to such frustrating experiences.

"Do you know where I can find the commissioner?" Malachi persisted.

"He has gone to the lower quarter," came a reply from somewhere behind the door. It was the voice of an older woman, a head servant perhaps. Malachi heard scuffling feet inside, and then the gate opened ponderously. "He left only a short time ago. You can ask for him there, but don't tell him I sent you. He doesn't like to be disturbed when he is down there." She appeared annoyed by Malachi's intrusion into her work, but when he handed her a coin, a faint smile crossed her face as she closed the gate.

The trip across town again was a short one. Malachi had no trouble finding the lower quarter. He simply followed the sloping city streets until the houses became more decrepit and scavenger dogs began to snarl at his presence.

And finding the commissioner was easier than he had thought it would be. Surprisingly, faces brightened when he mentioned the man's title. That's a bit odd, Malachi thought. The poor usually had nothing but disgust for the rich—especially the hated tax collectors.

Without a word, an old woman took Malachi by the hand. She escorted him down a narrow alley and into the doorway of a crumbling hovel that butted up against the city wall. Raw sewage pooled in the street in front of the house, and Malachi wondered if he would be able to stand the stench. Several men waited just outside the doorway.

A small flickering oil lamp sitting on the floor by a dirty old pallet struggled to relieve the darkness inside. Malachi squinted to let his eyes adjust to the gloom. On the pallet lay an old man, obviously extremely sick.

Kneeling beside him was the man Malachi had been searching for. It could be no other. His robes betrayed him, but he did not act like the wealthy man he clearly was. "How are you feeling, my friend?" Malachi heard him say.

Could it be possible? Malachi wondered. The wealthy avoided all contact with the destitute, especially someone so ill.

"I've been worried about you," the tax agent continued. "This is no place for an elderly man." Emotion filled the commissioner's voice. "I've brought you medicine and some food, but I'm not sure that's enough, now that I see your condition."

He smiled encouragingly at the wan face of the old man on his mat. "Obadiah, my friend, if Jesus of Nazareth were here, he would restore you to health—both in body and spirit." Patting the old man's shoulder, he added, "I guess the next-best thing we could probably do for you would be to take you out of here and get you some medical attention until you are back on your feet."

The commissioner paused as though deep in thought. "I should have thought to bring you to my own house long ago. That way I could have checked on you more easily and made sure you were getting well. Why not!" he exclaimed, delighted at a sudden bit of inspiration. "We can do it now. I have brought some of my servants with me—they can help move you and your things. Will you accept my invitation?"

The old man simply nodded as tears rolled down his leathery face. Within minutes the three servants had constructed a litter of sorts, and the old man was on his way with the men doing their best to keep him comfortable.

"Just take him on back to the servants quarters and tend to his most urgent needs before you do anything else," the tax agent instructed. "He will probably feel more at home there. Oh, and have Naomi tend to his bedsore right away."

The commissioner shook his head, then noticed Malachi standing in the doorway. "I can't believe I left him here this long," he told Malachi. "No one seems to care about the plight of the poor. It's a vicious circle. The poor can't get ahead because of their station in life, and because they can't improve their lives, they stay poor. And the rich don't help much," he continued, speaking to himself as much as to Malachi. "Keeping these people poor seems to be a game. Oh, we rich make a pretense at giving alms, but it's just one big charade."

As the commissioner left the hovel and began to wend his way slowly up the narrow alleyway, Malachi felt strangely drawn to the man. He was surprisingly friendly for someone of such high rank. Usually the rich were painfully snobbish. This one was charming, almost childlike in his magnetic ways. *There is something very special here,* Malachi thought. *It is almost as if the commissioner has a direct connection with heaven. Could it be possible?*

When they emerged from the lower quarter and into an open marketplace, Malachi found the courage to say, "My name is Malachi, son of Obed. I'm from Caesarea, and I've come to find Jesus of Nazareth, the miracle worker. I have been on this quest since last week, but I must say, I think I have nearly reached the end of my journey." Malachi stroked his beard. "I've already heard a bit of your story, but I wish to hear more."

The commissioner paused a second to study him. "Of course, Malachi. Anything to share the story of the Master. If you knew

Jesus, you would know that he transforms lives simply by looking at you. In a moment—in the twinkling of an eye—he takes the old and makes it new. Corruption gives way for a new heart—a heart of flesh." The commissioner pointed to his own chest for emphasis.

As he loosened the cords of his tunic belt he said, "I knew I would meet the teacher from Galilee some day. It was inevitable—he often came this way. The question was Did I really want to meet him? Although I knew of his incredible power to do amazing things, I was not sure that I believed him to be the Messiah. Jesus had a reputation for bringing transformation into people's lives in dramatic ways, and that scared me." The commissioner smiled sheepishly. "But he came, as I knew he must. It was almost as if he visited Jericho that day just for me."

A sudden commotion erupted in the marketplace, as though a whirlwind had come to town. A haggard-looking man burst through the city gate out of breath and heaving, as though he had been running for miles. The man fell to his hands and knees in the open marketplace. Between gasps of air he managed to exclaim, "There's been a crucifixion—three men were executed this morning at Golgotha." The messenger's labored breathing came more evenly now. "It was horrible, and Jesus—and—and Jesus of Nazareth was one of them."

A blanket of silence slowly settled on the marketplace as the realization of the announcement spread. The merchants, the vendors, even the Roman soldiers—all stood transfixed.

Malachi's legs began to feel weak at the news, until they finally buckled and he fell to his knees in the street. He swallowed hard to fight the scream of horror that threatened to escape his lips. This couldn't be happening. Not now. Not yet. The news destroyed everything that he had been planning and hoping for. It was as if the very earth had fallen away from under his feet.

To Malachi everything seemed as if in a dream—the marketplace, the animals standing with their loads, the dust hanging motionless in the afternoon air. He closed his eyes and shook his head. Could this be happening? The Romans conducted crucifixions from time to time, but only for hardened criminals and revolutionaries.

Surely Jesus was not a criminal. From everything that Malachi had heard, he was more saint than criminal. More God than man.

What had Jesus done wrong? No one seemed to know. The Romans would instantly destroy anyone that appeared to threaten them. Had he preached revolution?

The commissioner stood silent for several long moments before regaining his composure. "This is the worst news possible," he said in a state of shock. "I cannot believe it is true. There must be some mistake."

Almost in response to the commissioner's words, the messenger on his knees moaned, "It is true. I saw them pound the nails through his hands." The man bowed his head. "It was horrible for a man as good as he, and yet—yet through it all, Jesus of Nazareth did not curse them or plead for mercy. his only words were 'Forgive them, forgive them!' "

Shuddering, the messenger began to cry as if reliving the events. "Jesus was offering them forgiveness, but the soldiers and crowd mocked him!"

The commissioner found his voice again and laid a hand on Malachi's shoulder. "Please, my friend," he urged, "we must try to find consolation in the fact that the Master warned us this would eventually happen."

Malachi stared at the tax official incredulously. Consolation? What comfort could there be in that?

"He told us it must happen to complete prophecy," the commissioner tried to explain. "No one would listen at the time, but I am sure it is so. Somehow this tragedy must have meaning—at least we must accept it as so, for the time being, anyway."

The commissioner's words were subdued, but he clearly seemed in control of his emotions. It was as if a calm of heavenly assurance had settled upon him. But although he did his best to console Malachi, his words had little effect on the merchant.

Malachi stared at the official as if in a trance. Were the two of them really at the Jericho city gate? Was this blinding whirl in Malachi's head only a horrible nightmare?

"I must go!" Malachi stammered. "I must see Him before He

dies. I must see Jesus of Nazareth with my own eyes. I didn't believe soon enough, and now I am afraid it is too late—but—but if I go now, maybe I can see Him while He is yet conscious."

Malachi stumbled forward on the uneven paving stones of the street. Strange rumblings from beneath the ground caught his attention. He looked up at the sky now gray with a gathering storm, and he knew that it was somehow very fitting. Strange, though. The rainy season should be over.

Now life would never be the same. What had started out to be a week of great promise had ended with disaster. Malachi grimaced with pain. Evil men had killed a man of supernatural qualities. The horror of it all was too much for Malachi to fathom.

The tax official took Malachi's arm and steadied him. "My dear friend"—his genuine concern broke through the tangle of Malachi's thoughts—"you have been searching for truth, and you must continue to do so. God cannot abandon us. He never has, and he never will. You must put your faith in his divine promises and then leave the rest with him. He is our refuge and strength through every time of trouble."

The expression of peace in the commissioner's eyes amazed Malachi. It was as if nothing could shake his composure and confidence in God's goodness and omnipotence. Who was this man, that even the worst of times could not shake his faith in the God of Israel?

"Listen, my friend. If the Miracle Worker, as you have called him, could change me and make me a new man"—the commissioner placed his hand over his heart—"then He can do it for you. I was financially blind, spiritually poor. I was wretched in spirit and so far from the God of heaven that everyone here in Jericho had already consigned my soul to the fires of hell. But Jesus took this miserable piece of humanity and made me new."

The commissioner bowed his head humbly. "I may be short in stature, but I am not short on intelligence. The common sense he gave me and the power of his spirit has kept me searching for truth, and it has paid off." He smiled sheepishly again.

"The story your friend in Jerusalem told you of the short man called Zacchaeus is true. I am the abominable tax collector from

Jericho who gave his heart and his fortune to God—and I will follow him until I die."

Malachi swallowed hard and took a deep breath. "Will you go with me then, Zacchaeus? Will you go with me now and see this great man I have waited too long to meet? We can hire horses and an escort, but we'll have to hurry if we want to get there before Sabbath."

"I will go with you, Malachi, but we will not see a great man. We will see the Lamb of God slain for the sins of the world."

Chapter Nine

SABBATH

Pigeons skittered out of the pathway as Malachi paused at the entrance of the Antonia fortress courtyard. He paused a moment to catch his breath before gathering courage to speak to the Roman guard at the gate.

Had it really been worth all the effort? Malachi shook his head in bewilderment. What a sad turn of events this whole venture had turned out to be! He couldn't remember when he had been so discouraged. Just one short week ago he had been anticipating any news that might help him decide whether Jesus of Nazareth was indeed the long-awaited Messiah. With the passing of each day, each witness to the life and ministry of Jesus had sent Malachi's spirits soaring. Each new tale of wonder about the teacher and healer from Galilee had electrified him with the possibility that he might truly be the long-awaited one, the promised deliverer.

And then Malachi had heard of Jesus' crucifixion. He and the tax collector had raced back to the Jerusalem to the place of public Roman executions. Golgotha, they called it. They had barely reached it before the Romans removed the bodies. The sight had been a grueling one. Not only was Jesus of Nazareth on a cross, but also the thief Malachi had met a few days before in the Valley of Hinnom.

The prisoners had been stripped naked and hung on makeshift crosses. But Jesus was already dead, a fact that left Malachi speechless. Prisoners did not die quickly from crucifixion. The whole point of such a form of execution was to prolong the torture as long as possible and thus terrorize those who saw it. Some victims died from exposure to the heat or cold, but most from asphyxiation. The position they had been placed on the cross made it almost impossible to breathe without forcing themselves into a physically exhausting posture. Eventually the muscles of their diaphragm no longer had the strength to enable them to breathe.

And the two thieves on either side of Jesus were dead too—bludgeoned to death by the Roman soldiers. Broken legs always hastened the death of crucified criminals since they could no longer heave themselves up into a breathing position. The religious leaders, not wanting them still hanging on the cross when Sabbath began, had instructed the executioners to speed up the process of death. The stench of death hung about the place, and flies droned everywhere.

Malachi cringed at the cruel method of execution that Roman oppression used to terrorize Israel. He had seen crucifixions before, but he always avoided them. But this time it had been different. Jesus was supposed to be the Messiah! Respectfully, reverently, Malachi turned his face away from the sight. What a tragic day for the nation of Israel!

"Who was responsible for all of this?" he later remembered asking himself as some of Jesus' followers removed His body from the cross. Who would have to answer for such a heinous crime against a man said to be the greatest miracle worker ever seen in Israel? An angry mob, the Roman occupation government, the religious authorities? With every passing moment, Malachi found himself growing more and more livid with anger.

His plans for a future with Jesus as the Messiah had shattered into a million fragments. Now all Malachi could hope for was to pick up the salvaged pieces of the week and go on with his life. Go back to Caesarea and his business and try to reestablish some meaning in life, try to find hope in a future that looked bleak indeed. There was nothing else to do, unless . . . unless, of course, one considered the rumors—rumors that this Jesus would return somehow.

Where the rumors had started was anyone's guess. It was said that Jesus himself had warned His followers of His imminent death, but stressed that his execution would not be the end of everything. The tax commissioner from Jericho had said something about it, but where had he gotten his information? Maybe it was from those stories Jesus told—those parables. Jesus' closest disciples had vanished, gone into hiding. But it seemed that the religious leaders had asked the Romans to guard the tomb that another follower had given for His body to be buried in. Did that mean they were taking such rumors seriously?

But could anyone really put much stock in a rumor? It was easy enough for someone to prophesy their own death, Malachi reasoned, but after they died, those kinds of predictions usually perished with the person.

Whether or not the rumors could be substantiated, Malachi had to find the truth, and what better place to start, than with someone who had actually seen Him die? Despite the fact that it was the Sabbath, he spent much of the day searching the palace areas and the Antonia fortress to find someone who might know something. At last, spotting a solitary soldier eating his evening meal in a small alcove off the gate, Malachi cleared his throat and cautiously approached the lanky Roman sitting at a rough wooden table. "Excuse me, sir," he asked. "Are you the captain of the guard?"

The Roman put down the meat in his fingers and leaned back in his chair. "Who wants to know?"

"My name is Malachi." He bowed slightly as a sign of respect. "I'm a merchant from Caesarea, and I seek some information about Jesus of Nazareth, the teacher from Galilee."

The soldier wiped the back of his hand across his mouth. "The centurion you want to see is out right now. Titus is his name. He won't be back till later this evening." The Roman guard picked up another piece of meat and added nonchalantly, "As to this Jesus, I know little of him—only that he was crucified yesterday, and that he was a troublemaker." He stared suspiciously at Malachi. "Are you one of his followers?"

"I've never met him," Malachi replied truthfully, shaking his head.

The soldier thought a moment, then apparently decided Malachi was harmless. "You'll have to come back," he mumbled through bites of the greasy fowl.

"If you don't mind, I think I'll just sit here and wait." Malachi stepped toward a sack of charcoal leaning against the courtyard wall.

The guard glanced at him disdainfully. "Suit yourself," he growled.

It had been a warm day. Malachi settled himself on the bag of charcoal and mopped his forehead with a handkerchief. "I've gone through great effort to be able to speak with this centurion. Did you say his name was Titus?"

The guard ignored Malachi's aimless chattering in favor of his meal in front of him, but Malachi kept talking. "It seems as if I've been crisscrossing this city all day, and I just can't seem to locate him. I wanted to speak to Titus last night, but I wasn't able to find him then, either. I managed to contact one of the Jewish priests, and he said I would have to speak to the governor himself if I wanted any answers."

The guard stopped eating and dropped his meat onto the clay plate in front of him. As he stood he knocked his chair over. "Listen here," he snarled through mouthfuls of food, "you're not going to get an audience with the governor! Who do you think you are, anyway?" He wiped his mouth again with the back of his hand. "The governor has little enough time as it is to carry out his duties, without wasting it to speak to you about this *Jesus!"*

Malachi stared at the Roman. What had he said wrong? Everywhere he went he found that the name of Jesus stirred people up. Some reacted favorably; others grew hostile.

"What is all the commotion about?" a voice demanded from just beyond the gateway.

Prickles ran up and down Malachi's neck. Suddenly he realized that he just might be creating more trouble for himself than he really wanted. He could be facing danger, perhaps prison or who knew what else. If the Romans got the notion in their heads that he was a follower of Jesus, then maybe they might deal with him as they had Him.

A cold sweat began to creep over Malachi. He resisted the urge to glance furtively about him. Maybe it still wasn't too late to make his escape.

"Are you deaf, soldier? I said, what's all the commotion about?"

"Uh, I'm sorry, sir," the soldier replied to somebody inside the fortress. "Nothing to be concerned about here, sir!" The guard set his chair back on its legs and added, "It's just a man inquiring about Titus's assignment yesterday at the crucifixion of the three prisoners. He wants to speak to Titus about the prisoner from Galilee."

During the long pause Malachi wondered if the other Roman would have him arrested. Surely, whoever the person was, he would not care about Malachi's search for information on a dead man!

"Send him in," the voice finally said.

The guard and Malachi stared at each other in surprise for several long moments, but neither moved.

"I said, send him in!" came the voice again, now impatiently. "Do you understand an order when you hear one?"

The guard snapped to attention. "Uh, yes, sir! I mean, he'll be right in, sir!" The guard stepped to the open gate and motioned for Malachi to enter. He shook his head nervously and raised his hands helplessly before returning to his post of duty and his plate of meat.

Malachi stepped into the stone-paved courtyard. The walls of the fortress rose before him to the high towers overhead. In one swift glance he took in the parapet surrounding the high limestone walls, the pacing guards, and the standard of the Roman legion stationed there.

An imposing officer dressed in ceremonial armor stood over a ledger he was surveying with, what Malachi assumed was, a military clerk. As Malachi entered, the man glanced up momentarily. "I couldn't help overhearing your conversation with the guard outside. Perhaps I could be of help to you."

"Thank you, sir" was all Malachi could stammer. He had no idea what to expect. What the officer wanted with him was a mystery.

The officer made a few remarks about some numbers entered in the ledger and then turned to leave. "Why don't you come with me?" he gestured to Malachi. "Let's go into my chambers. We'll be able to talk there with fewer disruptions."

The two walked through a doorway and down a covered portico. They took two flights of stairs and then came to a curtained doorway guarded by two soldiers. Malachi had to hurry to keep up with the Roman.

Once inside, the man offered Malachi a seat and then sat down himself. Within moments a copper-skinned Egyptian girl entered the room. She carried a bronze tray with a pitcher on it and some fragrant spice cake. Another servant removed their sandals, and a third brought a platter of fruits. "Please," the officer invited, "enjoy some refreshments."

Malachi glanced around the room warily as he sipped his drink and nibbled on a slice of spice cake. What on earth could the Roman officer want with him here? He had hoped for a visit with Titus, the centurion, but evidently it was not to be. Although it appeared that he hadn't done anything too offensive so far, Malachi began to feel that it just might be best for him to apologize for the inconvenience he had caused the officer, and then politely leave.

The Roman took a fig cake from the fruit platter. "You want to know about Jesus of Nazareth." It was more of an announcement than a question. He bit into the fig, chewing the fruit meticulously as he looked intently at Malachi.

"Yes, thank you, Officer. I was hoping to find Titus, the centurion, to ask him about the execution and—Jesus of Nazareth."

The officer looked at Malachi solemnly. "Ah yes, Jesus of Nazareth." He sighed as his chin dropped to his chest. "My wife was right about him—I knew she was right. If only I had listened."

Puzzled, Malachi searched the man's face, trying to understand what the Roman was talking about.

"She's a remarkable women," he blurted. Then remembering Malachi's presence, he waved his hand to the side as if he couldn't possibly expect Malachi to understand what he was talking about. He shook his head dejectedly and turned to stare out the window. Malachi could hear a detachment of soldiers gathering in the courtyard below.

"Sometimes I wish that I had never aspired to the political arena," the officer sighed. "It can be such a risky profession. There're just too many factions and interests to appease and please and balance against each other. Each trying to get an advantage or destroy the other. Too many . . ." His voice trailed off and he glanced at Malachi who was feeling more and more confused.

"I'm sure you must be right," Malachi muttered, fervently wishing he could escape.

"It's uncanny, isn't it?" The officer had a droll look on his face as if he were trying to find some humor in a hopeless situation. "When one must make really important decisions for the gods and the empire, that is the day that everything falls apart. And those are the times when black and white begin to blur." He sighed again, and muttered an oath.

For the first time Malachi noticed how tired the Roman officer looked. Somehow he seemed older than he really must be. Malachi couldn't quite put his finger on what made him look so prematurely aged.

The officer clapped his hands to summon the servants again. "This Jesus of Nazareth," he continued as he took a cup of wine from a small tray held out by the servant girl, "he comes out of nowhere like some mythological character. He emerges for a few short years and thinks he will change the world forever!"

The officer gulped the wine down quickly, then wiped his mouth on a towel lying across the arm of his chair. "In these parts, one can never really take a religious teacher seriously," he added. "Not unless he is a zealot, or a religious bigot, or something." The officer helped himself to a few more figs.

"So, this Jesus of Nazareth," Malachi asked cautiously, "where does he fit in?" Malachi wasn't quite sure what kind of an answer he could expect from a Roman.

"I keep asking myself that question, but I'm sure I don't know. One day he's preaching kindness and love and good works for others, and the next, his followers are trying to crown him king." The officer gestured as though it were the most absurd thing he had ever heard. He laughed uneasily. "I'm sure you must understand that I can't permit this sort of thing to go on in the province of Judea. I mean, what would Caesar say? Jerusalem, hotbed of insurrection and political anarchy, bows to the will of a new self-proclaimed king. That's ludicrous!" The Roman spat the words out, but they seemed forced. Something else was frightening him even more.

"It's crazy!" He rolled his eyes in frustration. "Most prisoners that have to face me get down on their knees and grovel, begging for mercy, but not him. Do you know what this Jesus of Nazareth said to me? Here in my court, under my jurisdiction, while he stood bound and guarded? I had just reminded him that I have the authority to crucify him, and he had the gall to say, 'You would have no power over me if it had not been given to you from above.' Can you imagine that?" The officer's anger and frustration intensified. "I mean, was he talking about Rome, or was this power going to come from the gods, or what?

"I regret that I lost my temper and started mocking him. It was outrageous for Jesus to make such a claim and expect me just to look the other way! I don't care how much good he thinks he's doing in these parts; I can't have insurrection on my hands."

The officer shifted restlessly in his chair. "And of course I fully expected him to lose his temper and say something that would condemn him for sure. By then it was what I really wanted. Then I'd have a case against him and would not be just doing the dirty work for the local religious leaders. A way to eliminate some rival of theirs."

Beads of sweat began to collect on the man's face. "You know, it's strange, but for the most part the prisoner didn't say much." The Roman had begun to spit out the words faster and faster, as if he were defending himself before some tribunal. "What he did say"—the officer caught himself and forced himself to speak more slowly—"What he did say he said very solemnly and with great authority. He said, 'My kingdom is not of this world. If I had planned it otherwise, then my servants would fight.' Now, what did he mean by that?" Malachi bit his lip, hoping that the Roman would not expect him to actually answer his question. But the officer was still remembering the incident and oblivious to everything else.

"And then he started talking about truth. Truth! That was the last thing I wanted to hear." The officer shook his head vigorously for emphasis. "In the deepest recesses of my mind I think I already knew what real truth was—I could see it in his eyes." The Roman officer threw his hands up in a gesture of futility.

By now Malachi was beginning to panic. What if the Roman took his frustration out on him? But then he forced himself to remain calm. No, the truth about Jesus was exactly what Malachi wanted to find out, even if it obviously terrified the officer. That was precisely what Malachi saw in his eyes—fear. Fear, perhaps, that Jesus of Nazareth really was a threat to the officer, to the civil peace of Jerusalem, or perhaps even to Rome. What the officer was thinking, Malachi couldn't be sure, but he was positive that he had seen that look somewhere else recently. Had it flickered across the face of Caiaphas, the high priest, that day in the Temple?

A look of chagrin shadowed the Roman's face. "You know, it's strange," he sighed, "but Jesus didn't seem at all like those other revolutionaries and bandits plaguing the Empire around here. I noticed that immediately when we put him on trial! We followed the usual procedure for hardened criminals, but he didn't react like them." Shame filled the officer's voice. "But what kind of response did we get from him?" he asked in exasperation. "Only a few calm remarks and those penetrating looks of pity! He was the one who deserved pity!"

The officer gave a few feeble gestures of helplessness in the face of such unexplainable behavior. He shook his head in agitation and stared at Malachi in bewilderment. "The man had courage, I'll give him that much. He was on trial to be executed, yet he acted as if he felt sorry for me. I don't mind admitting that the whole thing made me feel terribly uncomfortable. It was if he was looking right through me. Unreal, I tell you! He didn't protest that he was innocent, that the trial was a mistake, as every other defendant does. It was—it was as if he knew exactly what was happening and wanted it to happen just the same. Almost as if he had a death wish."

The room was strangely quiet. "I'm sure you must know what we put him through," the officer muttered. Malachi wasn't sure he wanted to hear any more, but the Roman was speaking again, as though he needed to get a horrible nightmare off his chest.

"I didn't think I still had it in me to feel nauseous about a man suffering like that. But I will never forget it. Never! As long as there is breath in me, I'll vividly remember the cruel torture I put him through." He winced painfully.

Dark circles ringed the officer's sunken eyes as he raised his tired face to meet Malachi's silent gaze. "It was a revolting show those guards put on for one another. The mocking, the scourging. I ordered the scourging only to scare him into submission, and I don't know why I even allowed that! I shouldn't have. He didn't even resist!

"I've seen a lot of scourgings in my time," the Roman said slowly. "But there was something very strange about this one. Frightening. It was almost as if my soldiers had become inhuman.

No! I'd say it was more like—demon possession!" his voice raised with emphasis. "That's what it was! Demon possession—if you believe in demons. I can think of no other way to put it. It was as if unseen forces were at work in my court of law yesterday."

The statement left Malachi speechless. He had hoped to find the centurion and ask him questions about the final moments of Jesus' life, but he had not expected to encounter the person most responsible for Jesus' execution. Somehow he had always seen the Roman justice system as an inevitable force that rolled along and meted out the natural consequences for a life of crime. When someone committed a crime, the law had to be carried out, and that involved the courts and sometimes the death penalty. But in this case, justice hadn't been served. His heart told him that Jesus was innocent. He had to be! And this officer was to blame for the horrible miscarriage of justice.

Malachi's mind became a blur of jumbled thoughts and anger. By now the merchant hardly heard anything that the Roman said as he grappled with the horror of the whole incident.

The military officer got to his feet and went to the window to stare out on the lengthening shadows of the Temple complex below. His eyes got that faraway look again. "They're all saying that he was a Son of God—that he was no mere human being. I can't believe that any god would allow his own son to go through what Jesus of Nazareth went through. At least not those we Romans worship." It was almost as if he had forgotten Malachi's presence in the room.

For a long time the man said nothing. When he did speak again his voice was so subdued that Malachi could barely hear the words. "I would almost trade anything to do yesterday over again. But it's gone—and so is Jesus of Nazareth."

He glanced at Malachi furtively. "And do you know, the worst part of it all is that I'm afraid it's not over. Somehow in my heart I believe what Jesus said about his kingdom not being of this world. He may be out there in a tomb, but somehow I sense that I have not seen the last of him." The officer returned to his chair and slumped into it.

If it had been another time and place, Malachi might have felt sorry for the Roman official. But at the moment the merchant fought to hide his fury toward the Roman authority who had ordered the execution of Jesus of Nazareth. Although he wanted to strike out at the Roman prefect, he instead felt himself calming down, as though some unseen force had arrived to give him strength. It was as if Malachi had come to grips with reality and had resigned himself to the outcome. Nothing could be done about Jesus' death now.

A feeling of peace settled on him like a warm cloak on a chilly evening. Was it all coming together now? Everything Malachi had gleaned from witnesses during the past week had yielded the obvious—that Jesus of Nazareth was indeed the long-awaited Messiah. Malachi was sure that somehow Jesus' life and death were a part of God's salvation plan, and he was also sure that even now Jesus had just begun to work for his people. While Malachi couldn't quite fathom how this would all come about, something within him told him it was true.

As Malachi quietly slipped toward the door, the Roman official seemed to shrink within himself. "I tremble for tomorrow," the man said bitterly to himself. "I know already what it holds. Fear, I'm sure, will be my constant companion, and waiting somewhere in the future is my inevitable day of reckoning. It doesn't matter that I am the great Pontius Pilate, prefect of all Judea. I have been weighed in the balances—and I am found wanting."

Chapter Ten

SUNDAY

Malachi paused to tighten the leather straps that secured the load on his donkey. He checked to see that he had an ample supply of animal feed for the return journey to Caesarea. With a little grain once in the morning and then again at night, his donkey could manage by scrounging for grass along the road.

And now for a final stop to fill his waterskins. He preferred the clear water from the Spring of Gihon even if he did have to go a bit out of the way to get it. It did not have the stagnant taste of the cisterns in the city. Nor did he have to worry about something dead floating in it.

When he arrived at the enclosed stairwell that descended to the spring just inside the eastern city gate, scores were already waiting in line to fill their vessels. Some came with pots or jars atop their heads, mostly young girls sent by their mothers on the daily trek to fetch the family's supply of water. Others stood with their water skins tied to their belts.

Malachi knew he should have come earlier. He had wanted to put as many miles as possible behind him before the heat of the noonday sun made the trip uncomfortable, but the prospects for an early start were even more remote now.

His heart was heavy as he thought of all that had transpired since he had arrived in the city a little more than a week ago. So much had happened in such a short time. He had come to Judea in search of the Messiah, clinging to the hope that the much-acclaimed Jesus of Nazareth would indeed be the one for whom Israel had waited so long.

Malachi had to admit that his visit with Rabbi Simon on Sabbath had left him wondering. Why had the rabbi felt compelled to throw a feast in payment for Jesus' gift of healing? Wasn't God's gift of life free? The early-morning trip to see Lazarus had astonished Malachi, though it had made him want all the more to meet the miracle worker who could raise the dead. And then there had been the disappointing visit to the Temple on Monday. The chaos of the Temple animal market and his conversation with the high priest had left him confused again and a bit discouraged. By Tuesday Malachi was still searching, but he felt ill-prepared for his encounter with the thief in the Valley of Hinnom. The thief had probably gained more from their conversation than Malachi had.

The following day his encounter with the woman in the Temple court had revived his spirits. She had single-handedly helped to restore his desire to find Jesus. But it was the trips to Bethany and Jericho later in the week that had proved to be the highlight of Malachi's search. They had helped him crystallize his conviction that Jesus was indeed the long-awaited Messiah.

Unfortunately, tragedy had followed triumph. For Malachi, Friday afternoon had ended in heartbreak. The Roman authorities had crucified Jesus of Nazareth, devastating Malachi. It was as if Jesus' death had instantly shattered his dreams. The fact that he had never had the chance to meet Jesus for himself made the pain all the greater. The anger and fury he felt toward Jerusalem's religious leaders and the Roman prefect knew no bounds. If he could have, Malachi would have snatched them all from their places of power and self-importance. What a week it had been, and what a discouraging end to a search for the Messiah that had begun with such promise.

And now Malachi had to return home to Rachel and his children. He dreaded that moment, not because he didn't want to see them, but because of his own feelings. His disappointment would cast a cloud over the reunion. Maybe the two-day journey back to Caesarea would give his feelings time to heal. At least he hoped so.

Malachi shook himself to clear his mind of the stupor that had crept up on him. After standing in line for so long, he had just about decided to search for water elsewhere when a voice caught his attention.

"Would you like for me to fill your skins from my water jar?" The kind offer surprised him. She was a young woman, probably not more than 21 or 22 years of age. He had never seen her before, at least not that he could recall, but then it was Passover weekend and he was only a visitor in Jerusalem.

She deftly lowered the water jar from atop her head and quickly filled his two skins. He tied them off and then thanked her. She modestly accepted his offer of thanks and then turned to leave.

As Malachi watched her go, he wondered who she was. The woman had something strangely appealing about her. He felt a bit awkward and even a little guilty as his eyes followed her. It wasn't just that she was a woman, or the fact that she was beautiful. No, it was an aura that she carried with her. Suddenly he wanted to know more about her.

"Wait!" Malachi elbowed his way through the crowd milling about the spring.

The woman stopped and glanced behind her. Despite the fact that men generally avoided public contact with women in Jerusalem, she didn't appear surprised at his request—it was almost as if she had been expecting it.

"I want to thank you again for the water. That was a very kind thing for you to do. I would have had to wait for at least an hour to get water from the spring."

"I was glad to do it. It was the least I could do. You looked a little tired even at this early hour, and I think a bit discouraged. Is something troubling you?"

To his surprise Malachi felt himself wanting to tell her everything. About his trip to Jerusalem in search of the Messiah. About both his hopes and doubts of what he would find in the divine deliverer. About his elation at all he had learned about Jesus from those who knew him. And about the great sadness that threatened to ruin his reunion with his family when he returned home.

When he had finished, tears filled her eyes, but she still had a look of calm in the unblemished lines of her face. "What is your name?" she asked.

"Malachi."

"In the ancient language of our people your name means messenger—a messenger for God. No doubt God has great plans for you," she said, "so that you will indeed be a messenger for Him. He has been good to you, Malachi. The Lord has blessed you with a good wife and two children. The Father in heaven has been watching over you and helping to make your spiritual paths straight."

She studied him a moment. "Losing the opportunities you might have had to meet Jesus for yourself has been a hard lesson to learn," she continued, "and I think if you had it to do over, you would have searched Him out the first few hours you were in Jerusalem."

"I would have." Malachi grimaced even now at his failure. "I would have, but I have to be honest. A part of me is forever wanting to calculate every step of my life so that I will never have to step out in faith too far!"

"We all have parts of our life that we're not proud of, Malachi. That's reality, but what we do with those parts in the future is the most important thing, don't you think?"

Malachi knew she was right. She had to be right. It was the only thing that made sense at the moment—to him at least. "I went to a garden near the winepress beyond the Kidron Valley last night. I needed to go someplace where I could pray in private. A friend of mine suggested the spot. He said he goes there all the time now."

Suddenly Malachi worried that it all sounded like a confession, the way he said it, but the woman listened as though she had nothing else to do. He wondered who she might be. Was she a prophet? It was as if she knew his very thoughts.

"I just wish that I could have seen Jesus and talked with Him at least once," Malachi continued. "Why didn't He seek me out as He did so many others? He came to Lazarus and the tax commissioner in Jericho. Went right to Zacchaeus' house and invited Himself in for the evening meal. If only Jesus would have done that for me, then I would have had something to hold on to."

The woman was patient. "These men were blessed, Malachi. No one would take that from them. It's true that some of us must hear God's voice in order to be sure that He exists, and some must see the hand of God in order to believe that He answers prayer. However, you are neither of those types of people, Malachi. The Father will bless you even if you have not seen, yet still believe. This kind of faith is the greatest of all."

"I want to believe, good woman! I want to! Can you help me?" he begged. "I must do something, because I'm afraid it is going to crush out the little bit of faith that I still have!"

The young woman stared intently at him, then glanced through the city gate at the road now filling with pilgrims for the Passover festival. "You wish to take time for this now—shouldn't you be on your way? The sun is getting higher, and you have many miles to go."

Malachi took his donkey's lead rope and adjusted the halter, but hesitated only a moment. "I have time, and this is important to me."

"Then come with me. I want to show you something." They fell in step together as the road wound its way up the Kidron Valley. She walked easily with the water jar atop her head. It always amazed Malachi how the women could manage such a feat.

"Is that the garden where you prayed?" she said some minutes later, pointing to the shade of a grove of olive trees at the base of the Mount of Olives. "You know, Jesus himself prayed there the night of His betrayal, and it was there that a mob of evil men came to arrest Him."

Malachi, awed by the sacredness of the place, said nothing, but dutifully followed her lead to a family tomb not far from the place where Jesus had been crucified.

Solemnly they stood at the entrance of the grave where Jesus had been laid to rest, but to Malachi's surprise, the stone covering had been rolled to one side. He glanced at the woman for an explanation. "Wh—what has happened?" he stammered. "This is where Jesus was buried, isn't it? Have they moved the body?"

Suddenly Malachi felt a sense of indignation. He was aware that families sometimes did such a thing. They would rent space in a wealthy family's tomb and bury their loved one in it temporarily. Of course the plan was to move the body to a less-expensive location, but they almost always waited longer than this to make the switch. Malachi shook his head in disbelief. Jesus' body was gone.

Walking to the tomb entrance, Malachi bent over to look inside. "Where could they have taken the body? It's not still in there, is it?" He turned back to the young woman. "You don't think the grave has been robbed, do you?" Malachi knew it happened all the time, but what would Jesus have had on Him worth stealing? He was a poor man. And they would have left the body.

"It's quite plain and simple," she said with a smile. "Don't you see? He has risen."

Malachi stared back at her and stammered, "He has what?"

"He has risen. Jesus of Nazareth has risen, just as He said he would."

"Risen from the dead?"

"From the dead—in the flesh."

Malachi was all but speechless. "But—but how do you know? Did you see Him? Has He spoken to you?"

"He said He would rise again on the third day."

It was all Malachi could do to keep his composure. He didn't know whether to laugh or cry, to believe or to declare her claim a fraud and a hoax. "You know this to be sure?"

"I have been specially sent to you so that your faith in God's promises will be strong, and that you will know that your Redeemer lives."

As Malachi stared at her, a strange sensation began to creep over him as he dropped to one knee before her and bowed his head in reverence. Immediately she took his hand and raised him to his feet. "Please don't do that. I am just a fellow servant with you before the Father."

"But—I don't understand! This is all too much!"

"You don't have to understand it all right now, Malachi—just believe." She smiled at him again. "And one more thing—I have a personal message to you from Jesus himself. He has asked that you go on ahead of Him into Galilee. He will meet you there in three weeks' time, at a place that will be revealed to you shortly."

Never in his life had Malachi received such a shock to his system. The seesaw of emotions that he had experienced during the past 10 days of time had sent him from joy to desolation and back to euphoria again. For a long time he was speechless, but finally he found his voice. "Then, if God has sent you to speak words of encouragement to me, who are you?"

"I am a convert from a very long time ago, Malachi. I too was first a skeptic, then a believer. I became convinced that Jehovah was the one and only true God when I saw the miracles He was performing for His people. So it was either believe and receive salvation, or doubt and be swept away with the others. I chose to believe."

Her face was radiant. "I was not a good person, but God in His goodness has blessed me twice. Once when He saved my family and me at the battle of Jericho, and a second time when He raised me from my dusty grave this morning. I am a living, walking testimony of the power of the Father and His Son Jesus, who has also risen from the dead."

"It isn't possible—is it? You must be . . ." Malachi's voice trailed off in disbelief. He felt drained of all strength.

"That's right, Malachi. I'm Rahab." She bowed slightly and touched him on the elbow. "And now, I need to go, but may the God of Israel bless you in your newfound faith."

Chapter Eleven

THREE WEEKS LATER

It was already midmorning, and the crowds grew bigger with every passing minute. Excitement hovered in the air because it was rumored that the Master would meet with His followers again in this hallowed place. The grassy hillside slope overlooking the Sea of Tiberius lay just outside the city of Capernaum. Malachi knew that to many in the crowd the spot brought back unforgettable memories.

He recognized a few of those who had arrived for the reunion with Jesus. There was the group of disciples whom he had come to know since the Resurrection. All were there—except Judas, of course. Malachi had especially gotten to know the fishers among them, because he had already spent some nights fishing with them since his arrival in Galilee a few days before.

They included John and James, big strapping Peter, and of course his brother Andrew. Each did their best to introduce Malachi to the world of fishing, but it was no use. His arms just didn't have the strength to haul in the nets, and the fish smell was atrocious! It clung to his hands and clothes—Malachi knew that the pungent odor would linger on him for days.

But the companionship was good. The men argued among themselves as brothers typically do—not the bickering feuds that they had been accustomed to before they met Jesus, of course. Just good-natured tests of wit and brawn, bouts which the stronger among them usually won—Peter, more often than not. Malachi liked him. Usually Peter said what was on his mind, but when he had finished, that was the end of it.

And of course there were others at the hillside. Malachi had time to get reacquainted with Lazarus and his sisters, and the woman from the Temple who had spoken of her devotion to Jesus. And of course, there, sitting sedately among them all, was the tax commissioner from Jericho. Malachi loved the little man. Zacchaeus, who had been hated because of his role as tax collector for the Romans, had now earned great popularity through his Christian spirit.

Silas was there, and Malachi could hardly wait to hear more about his life-changing encounter with Jesus along the shores of this very lake. Even as they talked together, he could visualize the eastern shore of the lake several miles away. The sunlit slopes of the shoreline stretched inland to territory that he had never visited. Malachi wondered how many more thousands like Silas lived there without benefit of Jesus' teachings.

The very thought of it all made him shiver with sadness. Some, perhaps, would never hear of Jesus' life and resurrection. Malachi pondered that thought for a moment. Maybe it was up to Jesus' followers to take the news to such places as the countryside east of the lake. It made sense, if that was what Jesus wanted from them all. *H'mm, I guess we just need to wait and see what the future holds,* he thought to himself. *Jesus will have something to say about that, no doubt.*

Although Malachi looked for Rabbi Simon, he couldn't find him. "The Spirit of the Lord is upon him," he murmured to himself, "and sooner or later that imposing wall of reserve will come crashing down. He can't help accepting Jesus as the Messiah." The merchant smiled to himself. "I just hope it is sooner than later."

Malachi settled himself on a grassy knoll overlooking the shoreline not far below—he wanted to be one of the first to see Jesus when He arrived. Some of the disciples suggested that He would likely come by boat on the Sea of Tiberius. He had done it often before, and they had spent many a night with Him in such a craft. Others looked for His approach along the narrow rocky beach, and still others thought He might arrive from one of the smaller towns to the west—Nazareth or Cana, perhaps.

But no one questioned that He would come to Galilee. Had He not said that He would? Jesus was one to keep His word, to be sure. He might not always show up in the way some expected, and He might appear when they least expected Him, but He always honored His promise. From all that Malachi had learned during the few short weeks of his search, he knew this to be one of the constants in any relationship with Jesus.

Malachi smiled at the thought of that expression. Relationship. Although he had never met the miracle worker from Galilee, already he felt as if he'd known Him all his life.

And then suddenly, as if on cue, silence swept over the crowd of waiting disciples like an afternoon breeze in a field of wheat. Unexpectedly, and without great fanfare or ceremony, Jesus stood among them.

Malachi knew he shouldn't be surprised. He had come to learn that it was typical behavior for the Son of God. Jesus was the one person on the entire planet who had the right to come announced, to be proclaimed from the rooftops with trumpet calls, or to arrive via another triumphal ride on a noble steed. Yet He often made His appearance instead as a thief in the night.

It was obvious that these people loved Him—they worshiped Him. And why shouldn't they? He was their Savior.

The whole experience was almost eerie to Malachi. Here was someone who had died and then come back to life. Jesus walked among the disciples, greeting one and then another. It seemed that He had something to say to each one. Words of cheer, a smile, something personal that only the two of them knew about. He laid His hand of blessing on the cleaning woman who lived at the Temple. Next He embraced Lazarus, and it awed Malachi to see the two men together who had experienced both death and resurrection. But when Jesus came to Peter, the big fisherman dropped to his knees before the Master and began to sob as though his heart would break. Malachi didn't know the whole story, but he sensed the depth of their relationship.

And suddenly Jesus stood in front of Malachi. It was something the merchant hadn't expected or even anticipated. Jesus looked into his eyes, and it was as if He understood every thought, every notion that had ever entered Malachi's mind. While it was a humbling experience, one that bared the nakedness of Malachi's soul to its core, at the same time it was a private encounter shared only between Jesus and him.

Malachi had wanted proof that Jesus was indeed the Messiah—had all but demanded it. He had desired to see signs and miracles to help build his own faith in the unseen, but God had not honored those aspirations. And now all the small-mindedness, all the petty bigotry, brought on by his lack of faith was being exposed. All his resentment and jealousies and insecurities came to the surface for Jesus to see.

But somehow Malachi didn't mind. Instead, he felt safe here in the presence of Jesus, the one person he had needed all his life, but also the One he had avoided for too long.

Finally Jesus turned to the assembled crowd spread out along the grassy hillside of Galilee. "Peace be with you," came the clear resonating tones of His voice. He looked as Malachi imagined He would. Not because He resembled royalty. He did not. But the nobleness of His face and the searching gaze of His glance as His eyes swept the group gave Malachi the distinct impression that Jesus knew them well. Knew them better, even, than they did themselves.

The Master had much to say. His words were powerful beyond any Malachi had ever heard. "The half was not told me," he murmured to himself. Never had he heard anyone speak like this man! Jesus had the rapt attention of every person on the sloping Galilean hillside. He was inspiring, electrifying, and authoritative.

"Before you knew me, you did as you pleased," He said. "You went about your own business as though your lives depended on it. But now that you have grown spiritually, you are no longer spiritual children. From this day forward you have a much greater business to tend to—that of carrying the good news of the kingdom of God to every city and village and home. Feed my sheep—first in Jerusalem, and then in Samaria, and then to the most remote regions of the world."

Jesus' eyes swept from left to right. "But don't be afraid," He assured them. "I have traveled the road before you to prepare people's hearts to hear you, and some will quickly accept these words of life. Others will need more time, and by the grace of My Father in heaven, they will receive it. Some will join you and help to swell the ranks thirtyfold, sixtyfold, and even a hundredfold, but little or much, it matters not how many souls you win. It matters only that you be strong and of good courage, and that you do your best to let your light shine before humanity, so that they can see your good works and accept this message of eternal life. If others come after Me telling you of another way to accomplish this, don't believe it. They have been sent by the devil in sheep's clothing to become a snare to you and those you lead.

Jesus paused, and the light of heaven seemed to bathe His face. "Remember, this work is not yours, but that of My Father in heaven. If they reject you and the message of salvation that you bring, then they reject Him who sent Me." Sadness edged Jesus' voice. "Take little with you—no extra clothes, no food, and little money—but expect much from those to whom you minister. If they are not willing to share their hospitality with you, then they are not worthy of this gospel."

Jesus' words were gathering momentum now. "The world is our battleground, and on its fields you will be called to toil and sweat and bleed for the kingdom of God. Satan will give you great tribulations, but I am giving you ample warning here, today, so that when times of trial come upon you, you won't be surprised.

"These will be difficult times for you, but by God's grace you will be strong for the sake of truth. Some of you will be disowned by your friends and family. Like Me, some of you will be unjustly accused and dragged before magistrates, and governors, and kings. Others will be whipped and tortured and stoned, but don't be afraid, because in your hour of need I will be right beside you to give you the words you need to say to be My witnesses. When you are burned in the fire, or thrown to wild beasts, know that this is the work of the devil to crush God's people. Or when you must endure shipwreck, or sleepless nights on snowy mountaintops, remember, it is not in vain. Some of you will be martyred for the message you bring, but be faithful to death, and you will have a crown of life. Then when I come again the second time and make up the jewels of My kingdom, you will be there to shine as the stars forever."

For that one brief moment of time everything seemed to come to a standstill for Malachi. He didn't notice the bees moving among the last of the spring wildflowers that had carpeted the sloping hillside. Nor did he see the waterbirds gliding to a landing on the lake below him. Malachi was not even aware that the golden rays of the sun had broken through the patches of cloud in the late-afternoon sky. Only Jesus occupied the center of his attention right now, and that was enough.

The crowd, too, was transfixed—no one dared breathe, it seemed. Every eye and ear focused on Him. It was as if they were fearful that they might miss even one tiny morsel of the bread of life. His words were gold to them, a final parting gift coming straight from the mouth of God.

Jesus surveyed the crowd spread out before Him, and Malachi could see tears of love and compassion trickling down His bronzed cheeks. In a moment of sudden insight Malachi realized that Jesus' life and death had brought all these disciples together as children of the heavenly Father. Each was precious beyond measure in His eyes and the eyes of His Father.

Standing, Jesus raised His hands to the sky. "And now go, be My witnesses. Make disciples of all nations, baptizing them in the name of the Father, and the Son, and the Holy Spirit, teaching them to observe all things that I have commanded you. And don't forget—I am with you, even to the end of the age."

Malachi smiled to himself. That's exactly what he and the multitude of disciples on this grassy hillside were—witnesses. And they were witnesses, not only of Jesus' life and His execution on a cruel cross, but also His resurrection. And now, as disciples of the miracle teacher and healer from Galilee, they had a special invitation from the Son of God himself to take this vital message to all the world. A message of salvation and the good news that Jesus would return to take His followers to heaven with Him.

So Malachi had come to the end of his search. He had at last realized his heartfelt wish to see the Messiah—not in the way he had expected, but in a manner far and above what he could have possibly hoped for. Jesus of Nazareth, the miracle worker from Galilee, was indeed the Promised One. He was the Savior of the world and the Son of God.

19-183